*Palewell Press*

# Fur Beneath the Skin

A quest for identity

for young adults (17-21)

*Christie Dickason*

Fur Beneath the Skin
First edition 2020 from Palewell Press,
https://palewellpress.co.uk
Printed and bound in the UK
ISBN 978-1-911587-38-5

The front cover photograph of a forest at night,
downloaded from www.shutterstock.com, is
Copyright © 2020 miloszguz1[monkey]op.pl

The image of a wolf's head superimposed on the front
cover photograph was downloaded from www.canva.com

The photo of Christie Dickason is Copyright © 2020
Christie Dickason

The cover design is Copyright © 2020 Camilla Reeve

A CIP catalogue record for this title is available from the
British Library.

# Acknowledgements

My heartfelt thanks to:

Stephen Wyatt, who pays me the compliment of being honest.

John Faulkner, my husband, who lives with the 'wolf' and googles for me.

Tom and Marina (and Seb for keeping my spirits lifted).

And most of all, my publisher Palewell Press, whose chief editor Camilla Reeve knew what I was doing – a can't-put-it-down, page-turning historical novel told from the point of view of a boy who did not have the word yet in the 17th century to describe his state of being but now would be described as 'diverse'. Not a finger-wag but an exciting read.

# Dedication

For you.

# Foreword

I feel something stirring dangerously in my body.

Then I meet others who are different, like me.

Fear is our enemy.

One girl is not afraid.
The trouble is, she prefers me as a werewolf.

# 1

Cambridgeshire – 1604

*Deep in its shadows, my brain says I'm dreaming. My body says that this is real. They want to kill me!*

*I run naked across a dark ploughed field, stumbling on ridges of earth. My skin feels on fire. Boots thud behind me. I hear harsh ragged panting. I smell torches behind me, trailing flame threads and sparks. A hornet buzzes past my right shoulder. The explosion of musket fire catches up.*

*Black water ahead…irrigation ditch. I soar miraculously through the air, leaving the panting and the thudding boots behind me on the far side of the ditch.*

*I stretch to reach for the far bank but fall backwards. Mud grabs my feet. Dark water pulls me under.*

*Must breathe… surface again, breathe in beautiful air.*

*Gasping, I shake the water from my eyes. The smell of their torches is close to me now. Dark shapes loom above me on the bank I just left. One flings something into the air, hungry, covering the sky. I slip on wet grass. I struggle in the net. My arms and legs tangle in it. A shape*

*clambers down toward me. Raises its arm. I duck my*
*head uselessly. The night explodes into fragments of light.*

The breathing is near me.

I haul at my eyelids.

The breathing. In...out. In...out. In...

I must be dreaming that I woke up. I decide to stretch. Deliciously. Still half-asleep.

Can't stretch. Seem to be tied. In an uncomfortable position, on my side. I struggle. My lids jerk open.

I stare. The flared silver muzzle of a gun stares back at me, its eye black and steady.

I'm not dreaming. I'm naked, on my left side, on a cold, grey-blue stone floor flecked with ochre. My spine curls forwards, real pain from wrists and ankles lashed together, bent knees forced out on either side of my body. Doesn't make sense.

I can't believe it, but it's true.

I really smell cold dampness from the real stone floor. Yellow dust and straw and dark green horse dung, the blinding red stink of real fear. And the pungent acridness of garlic. My head throbs. I remember dreaming only that I ran and that the night exploded into light fragments.

My eyes are drawn helplessly back to the gun. Its dark eye still stares at me. A real gun, I decide.

None of it makes sense.

A band tightens around my chest. Still disbelieving, I tear my eyes away from the gun and see light brown raw wood walls, dark gold-brown hay in a black iron manger etched by red-brown rust. Shadowed beams are above me. From one hangs a huge, dark-brown and black padded leather collar marked by grey sweat lines. Its size says it is for a plough-horse. I seem to be chained in a barn, in a horse's stall.

My eyes return to the gun. The gun leads to a man, a rough necklace of garlic around his neck, three cloves of it pierced by a string.

What's going on, I try to ask. Why I am chained?

Words won't come. In the silence, a horse kicks its stall with a hollow wooden thump.

I shake away the fur muffling my thoughts but instead set off pain in my left temple. Heavy metal links of chains grate on the stone floor. I look.

They are my chains, attached to my bound ankles and wrists.

'Where am I?' I manage to croak at last. 'What am I doing here?'

'It's awake!' the man shouts. 'Get the others...! Quick! Don't leave me alone with it!' Footsteps leave at a run.

Startled, I try to turn to look behind me at whatever they caught when they chained me. 'What is it? Will it hurt me?' I ask him.

Then I realise. The gun is not aimed past me at something else. It is aimed at me.

But I'm not an 'it'. At least, I don't think so. I tear my eyes away from the gun and crane my neck to look down at my body, sideways on the floor. It looks strange without clothes on: long, bare, muscular shins and thighs; slim, bare, undoubtedly human feet, five reassuringly human toes on each. I peer: nails on both hands and feet gently curved, not very curved nor pointed. A bare human belly with a neat triangle of dark hair pointing up at my navel from a cock and balls nested in near-black fur.

Relief. Human and male. And young, to judge by my taut skin. The hair on my head that I can see by squinting is long, curly and dark. Not rough or bristly like dogs or cattle, nor sleek like a cat. I can't see my face but I'm reasonably certain it's human too.

I dig my thumbnail into my big toe to make certain I'm awake. I feel pain. The torch jumping in its holder makes it hard for me to think; I close my eyes while a wave of pain and giddiness passes. I rub my cheek against my shoulder and feel the slight growth of very new beard.

At least, I'm not an 'it' – I have the evidence of my own eyes. Not an 'it', whatever 'it' is. I lie curled like a grub on the cold stone floor, trying to remember how my face looks. With its new beard growth. Without some knowledge of how I look, I don't quite exist in my mind…I might have a very large nose or a little piggy one. I try to touch it to tell me but can't because my hands are chained to my feet. One eye might be lower than the other. My mouth might be…The possibilities expand.

I struggle against my chains, then sneak another look at the staring eye of the gun. As soon as I know what it is that I have to explain, they – whoever they are – will have to let me go.

All will be well, I reassure myself.

Heavy boots grit on the stone floor, accompanied by sour, dark alcohol fumes and panting. Five men carrying two more juddering, yellow-orange and blue torches come into the barn. All wear cloves of garlic strung around their necks. I count; they bring another musket, three wooden cudgels, a three-pronged iron hayfork.

I suddenly remember their dark shapes looming on the bank behind me. The thud and squelch of their boots. Their eyes beneath the broad hat brims had glinted in the torches that chased me through the dark.

I begin to accept that my flight in the dark was real. But it still makes no sense. I feel that I must seem human as possible and not the 'it', whatever it is, that my guard begged not to be left alone with. Grunting with pain, I roll up onto my buttocks. Still curled forwards, hands chained to ankles, knees bent up to either side, I peer up at the new arrivals. I would feel more human with clothes on but don't dare say it yet.

'These things...' says a loud, red-brown authoritative voice.

*These things?* I sit as upright as possible.

'...can steal your soul if you look them in the eye.' Seen from beneath my brows (which are dark brown, I think), he matches his voice, large and authoritative, with the ring of a final musical cadence.

'I am not...' I begin, but his heavy-soled muddy boots distract me. My hand goes to the side of my stomach; it still aches. But I can't remember why he kicked me. Careful now, I force my words to be respectful.

'Sir, you're making...' My mouth is dry. I swallow and try again. 'You're making a mistake, I'm not an "it", I'm...' My thoughts scatter and roll away like dried peas. Panic floods my chest and thighs. Not only my face but my name. I have lost my name.

'D'you hear how hoarse it is?' He is not listening to me. This time his voice is followed by several agreeing murmurs.

The pain in my left temple swells into a black cloud. *WHO AM I?*

My stomach heaves. I wipe my mouth against my knee.

'We've only bound it in its present form. What if it turns snake, for instance? And escapes. We don't know, do we?'

I grope for my name.

'Then what should we do, Master Grillet?' another voice asks.

Rafe! My name flows suddenly along the channel carved by another name. 'Rafe Seabright! Rafe. William. Seabright.' I say. Rich in my mouth like butter, more precious than pearls. I clutch it to me so it cannot escape again. My name. Tears of relief blur my sight. At last, now, they might see me as a fellow human. This whole dreadful misunderstanding will be sorted out.

Memories flood back with my name. I snatch at them.

Sixteen. I've just turned sixteen. Yes! A youth. Definitely human, definitely young, not an 'it'. Yes, yes! I'm not a shadow monster in a bad dream snapping its teeth as it runs. I have a sudden flash on a face – my face – reflected in water – somewhere – long nose, just losing its baby fat and acquiring a good jawline. I remember clearly: I set my jaw and watched the muscles bulge in front of my ears.

'I'm Rafe William Seabright.' I pin my name down. 'I ask your pardon for pointing it out, but you've made a huge mistake!'

Now they will take a second look. Even through their ale, they will see another human, like them. They will apologise. Or as close as they can come. They will set me free.

'Call yourself "Rafe William Seabright", do you? Remembered your name all of a sudden, have you?' Grillet's voice drips bile and disbelief. 'Then you'll no doubt remember how you slaughtered my best laying hen. Bit her head off, left her half-eaten, blood and feathers all over the ground!' He turns to the others. 'Chased a wolf, caught a man! I think we've caught us a werewolf!'

# 2

'A werewolf!' I suppress a snort. Though men their age accept werewolves, wizards and witches as part of their lives, I take pride in fighting my way out of such superstition. 'I'm not...'

'Wasn't it howling like a wolf? Grunting and growling in the dark in my orchard, blood smeared on its muzzle?'

Muzzle? My chains clank as I try to touch my nose again.

Heads nod. 'We heard him too...and saw.' Eyes slither towards me in frightened curiosity. Then, apparently not wanting to look me in the eye, they slide away again.

'...naked, on all fours, just like a wolf.'

'Biting the head off one of your hens revolts me! I don't even like the smell of blood.'

'Is that not the same creature we just chased and netted?' Grillet demands.

'Your orchard was dark,' says one of the others, perhaps more sober than the rest. 'I couldn't swear now on oath...those long legs... He looks human enough now in the light. And young and comely enough under all that dirt and blood.'

'There! Listen to him! I don't just look human, I *am* human! As human as you are! Human legs!' I haul against the chains and stretch out my fingers. 'Human hands. No claws. Look!'

'It's changed back into human form, you fool!' Grillet keeps ignoring me and talking to my defender. 'It's the same creature! How else do you explain that?'

He points at my right arm.

A long red weal of dried blood stands out on my bare arm among other scrapes and scratches.

'I'm covered with scratches!' I point out. Then I wonder how I got them all.

Grillet looks around, daring the other men to disagree with such proof. ''A "sympathetic wound." There! In the same place! Same wound on the same limb on this so-called "man" – I gave the beast in my orchard an identical one!'

Heads nod.

A new man enters the barn at a run. Panting and emotion makes his words ragged. 'My Alice…daughter… has disappeared!'

13

'Your daughter? We caught the werewolf that was killing my hens. Most likely killed her too.' Grillet points at me.

The new man turns on me, raising his arm.

'Easy, Brinkley!' Two men catch the arm of Alice's father just before the iron fish gaff he holds in his fist buries itself in my head.

Brinkley struggles to free his arm. My thoughts slither. A girl!

'Most likely ate her like my hen.' Grillet grins in triumph.

'Slit it open!' Alice's father yanks his arm free and fumbles at his waist. 'Do it now before its gut empties; you'll find what's left of her in its stomach.' He produces a knife.

An almost-memory flashes through my head and out again: spilling guts as neat as sausages. Somewhere.

Ice water begins to trickle into my belly. 'I swear I never touched her!'

'Let me go!' shouts Brinkley, struggling with the men who have grabbed him again. 'I'll show you...'

The ice water rises up into my throat making it harder and harder to breathe.

'We'll kill it, Brinkley, don't fear,' Grillet says, making common cause between a missing girl and a slaughtered hen. 'But in the right way, to prevent it coming back and taking its revenge.'

My heart lurches again.

'But I thought a devil can't die!' someone protests. Their voices begin to jumble in my head. '...needs a silver musket ball...Silver? Less costly to hang...'

The ice water fills me. I can't breathe. I don't remember killing, but these men are convinced I can kill. I don't remember last night. Running... the night exploding into fragments... that's all. Maybe I did bite the hen's head off.

'...burn them, just ashes left – no body for the demon to re-inhabit...throw it into a ditch and hold it under until...But who wants to hold down a...?'

The voice of Alice's father: 'I will hold it down, so long as it's done!'

Large pieces are missing. Memory slides away from me. Teeth snap...running. Ice chokes me. I can't remember last night. I forgot my own name, after all. Drunk or not, these men might not be mistaken. Werewolves are said to exist in the universe, as hard as I might resist the idea. I can't remember what I did last night. How can I argue with anything these men say? What if I did turn wolf and kill and eat the girl? What if I am a werewolf?

'I'll summon a priest,' says Grillet. 'He'll tell us the safest way to kill it.'

A priest will surely know whether I am a werewolf or not. It feels impossible, but what if I am? I will not think about the vivid colours and smells that I seem to have acquired.

# 3

The men leave. A new guard's gun stares at me while the man averts his eyes. A lantern moves in the shadows of the barn. I hear hoofs clopping on the stone floor. A pair of human legs is visible under a horse's belly as it is led out of the barn. Newly sharpened ears hear mutters and rustling in the courtyard outside. A horse's gallop fades slowly into the distance.

They must have sent for the priest.

I resist thinking about my new keenness of hearing.

I shift, seek a bearable position. I sit again and curl forwards on numb buttocks. Then lie on my right side again, my left side, my right side. The chains on my wrists and ankles cut into my flesh. My legs begin to ache fiercely. I want to tear them off.

*He will decide how to kill me. I must persuade him I am not a werewolf.*

I squeeze my eyes tight and try to catch hold of a memory to anchor me.

Those men speak English though not quite the way I learned it. I understand them, but I also speak...

I seize hold …Dutch. I also speak Dutch. I pull myself along a fragile rope.

*Don't jerk or it will break…*

Fragmented pictures suddenly appear in my head …concentrate on them...don't think about...*I live in Amsterdam...with my grandmother.* In two tiny rooms in Amsterdam, my life on the streets unknown to my grandmother. *Katryn the Corset...waves to me.* Signalling for me to come to her...and the other whores in the musicos. '*Alderliefest nachtegaal,*' she calls me. Dearest nightingale…

*The priest will decide how to...*

Another image, quickly. I see myself singing for the whores and their customers. The whores go about their work as I continue singing for them and their marks, so I have opportunity to watch them...

So how did I get here wherever it is...where they all speak English?

'Am I in England?' I ask my guard, unable to help myself. He tightens his lips and will not answer me.

The little window set high in the barn wall slowly lightens with the pre-dawn glow.

I will not sleep. Dying is absurdly impossible, but suddenly it's real. I can't breathe.

*What might be waiting for me? Burning...*

*Or drowning? What does it feel like to inhale water instead of air?*

I dig at my chains. They clink and grate on the stone floor. The eye of the gun never wavers. I stare back at it.

A minor-key bell clangs overhead. I struggle in panic to full consciousness. It's suddenly daylight. A pair of dirty dark brown wooden clogs stands by my head. Above the clogs is an apron flecked with damp, black-and-white chicken pin feathers. Above the apron is a bosom, covered in muslin and brown homespun. Then I see blue eyes assessing me.

The girl looks disappointed.

I curl to try to hide my nakedness. 'Sorry if I look human,' I mutter. 'Did you hope to see something different?'

The guard's voice: 'Get out, all of you! It's eaten Alice Brinkley already! D'you want to make it four more?'

She is the first person in this bad dream of England (perhaps) who doesn't seem afraid of me. I look back at her bosom. She has just swollen into a woman. Fair hair falls in darker damp curls over a smooth high forehead. I notice a delicious shadow cast by her full lower lip onto the upper curve of a rounded chin.

Beyond her, three full-grown women stare at me from a safe distance in the barn door.

'What these things most relish is human flesh!' The large woman who speaks has a square, red, doughy face. She stands in front of the other two and wears a food-stained linen apron, holding a carving knife in her fist and smelling of wood smoke and roast meats. She points her chin at me but aims her voice at the girl in my stall. 'It will enjoy chewing on hers if she gets any closer! Oh, but then, I forgot, she's the spawn of the devil. Maybe it won't eat its own kind.'

The other two women titter uneasily.

The girl in the feather-flecked apron ignores her. She continues to eye me with obvious disappointment.

'Come to gawp at the monster?' I ask her. 'I hope they made you pay well for the entertainment!'

'Don't catch its eye!' says the first woman.

The girl ignores her. Hand on hip, she frowns. 'After all that women's squawk in the kitchen about werewolves, I hoped at least for red eyes, bloody fangs, claws and bristling fur. Do you even slaver?' She speaks accusingly. As with the others, I can just understand her English.

'Let her feed that thing if she dares!' says the first woman.

'Do you trust them shackles?' asks the second nervously, also wearing a food-stained apron.

The third woman peers from behind the other two. 'My husband told me last night it had blood on its claws – that poor girl's, for sure.' Her dairy-maid smell of sour milk reaches my nose.

'Did they find Alice's body yet?' asks a small boy staring at me from behind the women.

'It ate her, you looby,' the first woman says with authority. 'A creature like that one over there first drinks its victim's blood then swallows the rest whole. Her body's inside its belly... What are you doing out here, anyway? Back with you and keep turning the spit – meat's most likely burnt on one side already.'

The boy leaves reluctantly, staring at me over his shoulder.

'I'm warning you!' says the guard.

After a final glance at me, the three women disappear.

'How can you tear apart a chicken and a child and stay so clean?' The girl sounds angry. 'What blood I can see looks like it's from that gash on your head. Still, everyone seems to believe...You may have to do. Breakfast?' She holds out a small basket in a strong, fine-boned hand. Without waiting for an answer, she kneels beside me in a pool of apron, linen petticoat and rough brown wool skirt smelling of sheep.

'Do for what?'

Ignoring both me and the increasingly agitated guard, the girl begins to unpack the basket.

I smell the damp black and white chicken feathers that fleck her homespun skirt and coarse apron. And yeasty, freshly baked bread. I remember the words of the first woman, 'spawn of the devil'.

Can the girl be some kind of demon? Would she recognise a werewolf? Would she help me escape if I were one? I don't know what I am anymore.

'If you've just eaten Alice Brinkley,' she says briskly, 'you won't be hungry for what I've brought...don't glare as if I just insulted you!'

'Aren't you afraid?'

'Not even when you glare at me like that.' Our eyes meet in mutual challenge. She tilts her head to the sound of the horses left in the barn munching tranquilly on their hay. 'Even the scent of a strange dog sends them wild. I fear danger as much as they do.'

'Please tell my captors! I wish they were as convinced.'

She snorts. 'I'm glad they aren't.'

And clearly has no desire to convince them otherwise.

Anger squeezes my throat. She is disappointed in me. She wishes I were an obvious werewolf with bloody fangs and claws – and she won't deign to say why. Struggling to sit, I scowl at her, this foolish girl, all unshared purpose and level blue eyes. Which, I notice, keep lingering on the shadows between my legs. I scowl at the basket. How does she imagine I will be able to eat tied like this?

'It's only bread, cheese, and ale. I fear we've run out of children and hens.'

I fumble for a suitably scathing reply. Then I see that she's looking at my chains and may be making an awkward jest.

We glance at the same time at the guard. He now watches both of us with equal suspicion. Our glances collide again.

She looks away and is busy for a long time uncorking a grey stoneware bottle from the basket.

'You must feed me.' I say, stating the obvious. 'I promise I won't bite off your hand!'

'It's not your teeth...' She takes a deep breath, shuffles closer to me, and holds the bottle to my mouth.

I gulp the watered beer. I have not drunk at least since opening my eyes to the gun, perhaps for longer, though I don't remember.

'You tug like a hand-fed lamb,' she observes, 'when its mother refuses it or has died giving birth.'

When I can draw only air from the bottle, she holds to my mouth a thick slice of fresh bread.

The delicious smell of yeast and warm wood-fired oven brings a rush of hunger that overwhelms even my awareness of being naked. I tear at the bread and gulp it down half-chewed.

'I'm hand-feeding a werewolf.' She has been watching my mouth. 'Not a fang in sight, more's the pity.'

'Forgive me for looking human.' I mumble. In spite of my renewed hunger, I pull back my lips, taking great care not to hurt her as I take another bite of the bread. I smell raw onions on her hand and apples. The odd dankness of wet feathers rises from her apron. I swallow the bite of bread and inhale deeply. Under the wool of her dress, I smell the warm, sweet, sweaty scent of her body.

All at once, in addition to fear and hunger, I am hit by a deep sense of loss.

She narrows her eyes. 'If I squinny, you could look a little like the wolf I once saw in a travelling menagerie – same odd amber eyes with darker flecks in them. Same nearly-black brows...' She starts to say more, changes her mind. I imagine that she sounds a little more friendly.

Then she flushes and leans closer. 'If you are an ignorant, superstitious country looby like that guard over there,' she murmurs, 'you might – in the darkness – take that long straight nose for a muzzle. And jump to the wrong conclusions about those long legs and arms.'

I want to ask her to rub those long, cramping legs but do not dare.

She begins to break some pale yellow, crumbly cheese into pieces. 'Do you have a name? Or don't werewolves have them?'

I open my mouth. Then I close it in case my name escapes again. But it comes to my tongue as if it had never disappeared. 'Rafe Seabright'.

'I hear a foreign land in your speech.'

'I think I live in Amsterdam, but I'm English...I'm almost certain.'

The blue eyes survey me.

'These "country loobies", as you call them, are very certain that I'm a werewolf.' I nod towards the guard.

'You sound as if you believe them.'

I look away, thinking of the disappearance of Alice Brinkley.

'Are you a werewolf?'

'I don't know!'

'You must know!'

'How? When I don't remember last night?'

'Don't shout at me! They're superstitious ignorant louts. You don't have to believe what they say!'

'They have the guns and chains,' I say. 'And the witnesses.' I glance at the guard. 'And I know myself that something is going on! I just don't know what.' I glare at her, dark brows furled. I dig the points of my elbows into my calves. 'Where did you learn such disdain for them?'

As if by magic, her English changes. 'I'm not one of them,' she says. 'I'm from London, was a Londoner till I was eight.'

'Is that a London accent?' I can't yet think why – if I can ever think straight again – she might help me after all. Lightness fills me.

She nods. 'I was too young to understand my mistake in charming Master Grillet into buying my indenture – my labour on this estate – from the Foundlings' Hospital in London. I could be very charming when I was eight.'

She glances away. 'I thought I knew everything then...Children don't know...Misjudged. Hadn't thought ahead to starting to develop...Anyway...'

I feel her let out a long, shaky breath.

She brushes crumbs of crust off her skirt as if brushing away her thoughts. 'I still don't think as they do here on this estate and never will. I just sound like them to avoid attention.'

She holds a piece of cheese to my mouth, ending the conversation.

I smell sheep's cheese, stronger than the onions and apples on her hand. My teeth close on it as softly as if trying not to break an egg. I swallow the questions I want to ask. She has confirmed England, at least.

'Do werewolves eat cheese?' she asks.

My eyes slide sideways at her. 'What if I said that, in spite of myself, I might turn into something that will kill you?'

She goes still as she studies me. We stare at each other. 'You wouldn't.'

'That's enough!' The guard jerks the muzzle of his gun towards the barn door. 'Back to the kitchen, witch girl! Now!'

She repacks the basket with defiant slowness. She stands, the pool of wool becoming a skirt and apron again. 'You've missed your chance to make them all happy by eating me,' she says in her London voice. As she passes the guard, she says loudly in the original, barely intelligible, local speech, 'Alice Brinkley most likely ran off to avoid another beating by her father. And any dog or a fox could have killed Master Grillet's hen.' She crosses to the barn door. 'These farmers fear what they don't understand and imagine an explanation.' She disappears. I listen to her footsteps fade across the cobbles of the barnyard.

I have not begged her for help. I don't even know her name. But whatever her secret purpose is in wishing me to be a werewolf, her disbelief in my possible demon cheers me unreasonably.

But, the more I think, the more I believe that she is wrong. My senses are now unnaturally sharpened like a dog. Or a wolf. The snapping teeth...something arrived in me, beyond doubt, then wiped out all memory of what I did while it was in me.

I listen to the noises outside the barn. A churn thumps and splashes monotonously. Chickens battle-squawk over scraps thrown to them, I hear the voice of a girl feeding them. Lambs bleat in the distance. Heavy boots pass in the farmyard. A bell clangs for mid-day. Cows lumber heavily through the yard to be milked, lowing in discomfort. Country sounds. Not the familiar noises of Amsterdam – vendors calling their wares, the underlying rumble of crowds pierced by occasional high shouts, competing church bells. Buckets of water sloshing over cobbles and a multitude of brooms fussing and scratching.

I smell in my imagination the stink of sewage in the canals, the stench of rotting cabbage from the market, the damp sour sheep tang of wool clothes that our little coal fire could never quite get dry, the oppressive odour of the two tiny rooms in Amsterdam shared with my grandmother.

Our clothes...My grandmother's and mine...I see them in my head.

The single estate bell overhead suddenly clangs in a minor key, jolting me back to the present. My guard lights a candle lantern and hangs it on a peg on one of the uprights of the barn. I close my eyes against the flickering light.

Have I really become a monster that could kill a child? How can I argue that I did not? Will a priest be able to tell what is true? When will he arrive? How much longer do I have on this earth?

I beg the girl in the feather-flecked apron to come back and tell me I do not deserve to die.

The evening air grows chilly and damp. Don't know what month. Sometime in the spring to judge by the lambs bleating in the distance.

30

I watch a new man take over as my guard, muttering in a huddle with the former one, snatching glances at me. After the first has left, he leaves the upturned barrel of the guard's seat for a soft pile of saddlecloths against the wall. We listen to each other breathing. Then he begins to snore. At last, the gun sags and stops staring at me.

Sleepy birds stir in the rafters. Mice and rats scuttle across the floor. Horses thump in their stalls. My body has turned from a single ache into being on fire.

I raise my head. My heart begins to hammer.

The girl slips into my stall from the shadows, bringing her scent with her.

'How did you get in?' I whisper.

'Secret way, hole in tack room wall. Can't stay long.' She carries a rough horse blanket. 'The priest has arrived. An exorcist. He will see you after he has supper and rests from his ride.'

I might not see another dawn.

She lays the blanket around my bare shoulders. 'I'm Kat, by the way.' She squats in front of me. 'Hello, wolf.'

My heart thuds even harder against my ribs. 'You shouldn't have come back!'

She holds out a smooth, strong young arm that gleams in the lantern light. 'I want to be certain what you are. Look. No bumps!' She turns her arm. 'Evidence that you are not a monster. Master Grillet frightens me far more than you do...makes my neck prickle and my arms come up in goose bumps when he stares at me a certain way when he meets me alone.' She leans forward to put her forearm within reach of my hands. 'Go on. Feel. No bumps.'

I stretch my fingers to touch her but curl them again. The sight and smell of her so close to me makes me feel hollow with loss. I am going to die without knowing what it feels like to act the man. I can't even touch her and feel it.

'Bite me!' She presses the side of her hand against my lips. Her skin is warm on my mouth.

I close my eyes but don't open my teeth.

She presses harder. 'Go on! Prove that you're some kind of wolf!'

In spite of myself, with eyes open and locked on hers, I part my jaws. I feel the shock of my warm tongue against the side of her hand. I close my lips on her flesh. The sharp points of my dog teeth dent her skin. My nose is filled with her scent.

'Go on!' she whispers. 'If you are truly a werewolf, bite me.'

My jaws quivers. I taste her flesh with my tongue. I groan and jerk my head away. 'I want to. So much!' Two yellow points of torchlight reflect in my eyes.

'"Wanting to" does not make you a werewolf! It makes you like other men, and, believe me, I know!' Her whisper is fierce. 'The blow that bloodied your head has addled your brain...I must go before I am missed.'

'Stay with me! Please! While I wait for the priest. I'll go mad else!' My voice rises.

The guard jerks upright and shakes his head to clear it, looking wildly around him as if to say he has never been asleep at all.

Kat ducks and pulls the horse blanket over both of us, her hand braced on the floor between my legs, her face pressed against my chest. We do not move. Her warmth leans against me. My nose is filled with her sweet, sweaty smell.

The guard's clothes rustle as he shifts position. Then we hear the silence as he listens.

Our two silences listen to each other.

I stir so that my chains rattle and begin to breathe heavily as if asleep.

After a moment, we hear another rustle as the guard leans back against the wall. After a few more moments. he begins to snore again.

Between edges of the blanket, I see the gun twitch in his hands. I watch a little longer to see if he is using the same trick I did. At last, I nod.

Kat pulls back. She eyes me and swallows. 'It seemed so clear before I saw you…before we spoke. Now I can't decide what to do.' She is silent for a while. Finally she murmurs, 'How shall we fill this impossible time?'

Without her cheek against it, my skin feels cold and exposed. But at least, she is staying with me.

What can't you decide, I want to ask. Why don't you fear me? The questions jam in my mouth. I want to cram in everything about her. I want days and months to learn, not a finite number of heartbeats. I imagine that she seems as reluctant to leave me as I am to have her go.

'I wanted to use…' She swallows again. 'Now I don't know…' A shiver shakes her body.

We stare at each other. The guard still snores on his pile of blankets.

'Your turn now to confess,' she whispers.

'Confess'. The word blossoms in my mind, driving out all other thoughts. The words of Latin prayers fall into my head...*Pater noster qui es in caelis*. Our Father which art in heaven. I smell in my mind the incense that always lingers in church air, in Amsterdam, the sandalwood from the priest's robes invisible behind the confessional grille. With that knowledge come more memories.

I suddenly remember why I am here in England. I remember that now. But I can't decide how to tell her.

'I have a mission...' I begin. Then try again. 'I am not Church of England.' Now the accepted English religion, decreed by the old Queen's father, Henry VIII, who wanted to be head of the church instead of the Pope in Rome. 'My grandparents refused to change their religion and follow King Henry. I was raised a Papist, remained faithful to the Roman Pope. I grew up in religious exile in Amsterdam.'

I wait for Kat to think it through and to recoil from a heretic Papist Catholic.

35

'I am a Papist,' I repeat in case she does not understand. 'Here in England. My grandmother fled to Amsterdam with my father after my grandfather was…killed. My father died of swamp fever shortly after I was born there. I don't think I've ever been in England before.'

She lays her hand over one of mine. 'I hope you don't mean to alarm me. I'm spawn of the devil, remember?'

We look at her hand on mine. She takes it off again.

'Grandmother was the only family I knew.' She is now as clear in my memory as if she stood before me in the barn: fierce, and slim in old age. Spun-sugar hair. Vain about her persisting beauty but she hid her hands, scarred and stained by the leatherwork done to raise me.

With a glance at the sleeping guard, I continue in a murmur. 'I always addressed her as "Madame" like the grand lady she was, once. She raised me in a land and language not our own, as she kept on telling me.' I speak quickly, leaving no space for thoughts of my future and what England might now hold for me.

'She scolded me when I ate with my fingers without wiping them. "You, of all people, must know how to behave." Her words rolled off me. She didn't know the half of it. Out in the streets, I was a street rat, spoke vulgar Dutch, had friends she knew nothing about.' I don't tell Kat that I trusted grandmother to love me dearly and that her severity, including the beatings, had masked her fears for me.

I don't tell Kat, either, that I earned secret money by singing for Katryn the Corset and the other whores in musicos and brothels. However, I could not resist boasting a little to offset my chains and admission of 'street rat'.

'She never stopped telling me that I was an English gentleman, even though I had never seen England and lived in a Dutch slum.'

'A gentleman?' Kat goes still.

'She made me learn English, French and Latin...'

'To read and write?'

I nod.

'French and Latin...' Kat murmurs unhappily. 'I never learned to read even English.'

I notice her discomfort but blunder on. 'It seems that I'm both a gentleman and a landowner.' I shake my head, caught between showing off to Kat and wry disbelief. 'The rightful heir to...an English estate.' Whatever its name was.

'"Never let yourself be pulled down to the level of street scum," my grandmother kept saying. How could I tell her I was already street scum? It seems that a place I've never seen and can't remember the name of is where I truly belong.' I can't resist a final flourish. 'As a landowner I can also become a knight or a minister of parliament.' I bare my teeth in a mock snarl. 'Not likely now, is it?'

Kat ignores my feeble attempt at humour and pulls me away from dangerous thoughts of later. 'Why did she leave if England was so wonderful?' Though our heads are still close in the darkness under the blanket, she has curled her arms around drawn-up knees. I feel distance growing between us.

'She had to flee. Being Catholic in the old style was dangerous here in England.'

'Worse than being a werewolf?'

'Just as dangerous, I think, at least in those days. All who remained true to the old religion were branded "traitors".'

The English could be condemned, grandmother had said, merely for continuing to believe as they, and their parents, grandparents, great-grandparents and great great-grandparents had believed before them.

'It's different now, with King James from Scotland on the throne with his Catholic queen. That's why I dared come to England.'

'If it's so much safer, why didn't she come back too?'

'She died.' The recent memory is still too raw to say more, even to Kat. The scene has sharp-edges like broken glass.

Just three weeks before, when I had just turned sixteen, my grandmother began to drown in her own phlegm.

Kat is waiting for me to speak again, but I can't get the words out.

Water rose in my grandmother's lungs day by day. Her voice dwindled, scraping out of her throat like a breeze through dry twigs. When she sucked at the air, I could hear a thick boiling in her frail chest. I gave all the secret money I had earned in the musicos to two doctors, who came to our two tiny rooms, bled her, held flasks of her urine to the light, then shrugged. I left our lodgings only to sprint for food. I dozed in my chair at night and jerked awake at every silence, hanging over her, unable to draw my own breath until she heaved and sucked at the air again.

I drop my face to hide it.

One week later, my grandmother pushed away the cup I was holding to her mouth. 'Well, I can't do it, so you will have to,' she had said firmly.

I had withdrawn the cup, not certain whether she was raving.

'Take that money hidden behind some loose bricks in the fireplace...Where is my crucifix?' She fumbled in the bedclothes.

'I swore on a Cross to carry out a mission...' I say now to Kat then sink again into memory.

Grandmother's search of the bedclothes grew more frantic. The breath gurgled in her throat. 'Where is it...? Where...?' Her voice grew thinner. She was wearing herself out with looking, visibly moving a little closer to death.

I had drawn a sharp breath. 'She had long ago pawned the small jewelled rosary and crucifix she smuggled out of England,' I say to Kat. 'In a panic to stop her frantic search of the bedclothes, I held my dagger so that the hilt and handle made a cross.'

She had reached out to touch it. 'Swear…' She paused, gasping for breath. '… by this Cross…after I die…don't protest…you will return to England, with its new Scottish King James who tolerates the old Catholics once more…'

She had gasped again. 'In Lincolnshire…on the coast…our home for seven generations…your rightful home.'

She was in earnest. I could not dismiss what she said. 'Say it!' she had ordered. Her breath collapsed into a thin wheeze.

'I came to England…' I now mutter. 'My mission, to claim…'

I still can't believe that I am the owner, somewhere, of grazing land, arable fields, fishing rights, and kitchen gardens. Nor that orchards, belonging to me, are in bud at this very moment, and in the autumn they will hang with jewel-like apples, pears and plums. That a ring of six different, distant church bells will carry across the fields in place of the out-of-tune cacophony of the Amsterdam bells.

I remember my grandmother tugging my sleeve to pull me closer as if an English spy lurked in our two small, smelly rooms. 'There's more,' she had wheezed. 'Now that England has a new king and a Catholic queen, it is safe to tell you my secret. I buried the family treasures on the estate before I left...hoped to return together.' She sucked at the air. 'Now you alone...'

'No! You'll recover!' I remember saying.

She had gone on as if I had not spoken. '...must dig up the gold and pewter and silver plate...lift them into the light again.' She had to work to speak each word. 'Put them back where they belong. Replace the great gold crucifix with the four saints in their golden gardens on the altar in the family chapel...'

Four saints, golden gardens, I remember repeating silently after her.

'...Do it for me, for your grandfather, for your poor dead father, for all our family before us.' Then she had slumped back on her pillows and smiled. 'At last, you will see my favourite chamber in the tower on a corner of a great, high-ceilinged central hall, with garlands of flowers painted on the beams. Your father was born in that room. Your children will be born there.'

I can't do it! I had cried silently. Don't ask me to do the impossible. How can I run an estate, even if I manage to find it? I'm Dutch street scum. Your former world is not mine.

'Swear to do it!'

Anything to stop that dreadful wheezing in her lungs.

I had sworn, in spite of being overwhelmed by the reality of what I had just promised.

'To claim...?' prompts Kat now, when I've not said anything for a while.

'Reclaim the family home.'

Somewhere on the coast in Lincolnshire, wherever that was.

My grandmother had stared at me then and covered her face. 'Where is my husband when I need him most? Where is he? Where are we? I want to go back home!'

'Where exactly must I dig?' I had asked desperately. 'What is the estate called? Madame...'

'Take me there at once! And don't tell me the coach journey is too long!' She fell asleep suddenly, worn out by talking.

Then I had realised that her eyes were open again and fixed on me. All her dwindling force beamed through them into me. 'Seabright Hall. Dig where sheep shelter.'

I had nodded. A great weight settled on my head.

Grandmother sighed and closed her eyes again.

Silence went on and on.

'Breathe!' I prodded her shoulder.

I lit a precious candle at the fire and took it back to the bed. She stared at me from under half-closed lids. The silence continued.

I shook her violently. The silence went on.

Voices in the street outside wove themselves into a raucous shell around the silent void where I stood.

'I was alone,' I murmur to Kat, 'in the only country I knew, but where she never stopped telling me I did not belong. I had just promised go to a strange country across the sea, where she said I did belong. She told me all my life that I was an outsider, an intruder, but made me vow to claim a place as my own that I'd never seen in a country I'd never been to before.'

'Didn't you think of breaking your vow?' whispers Kat.

'Of course! Then I thought, why not try to do as she asked? As an adventure. I know the name of the estate –

Seabright Hall – and roughly its location. What really keeps me in Amsterdam any longer?'

'So you're not Dutch street scum?' Kat pushes back the blanket. 'I must go. They will notice for certain that I'm gone.'

Something has definitely changed between us. It takes all my will to say the words I had been putting off. 'Run! Save yourself at least.'

'You're a gentleman, even if you half-believe you're a werewolf! ' She stands up uncertainly, with one eye on the guard. 'You have an estate to claim. Do what you can to honour your vow.'

We can't part like this. Forever, all jagged edges and awkwardness.

'Kat, you're my only friend in England. Have I offended you in some way?'

She exhales hard and reaches down to touch my face. I press my cheek against her open palm. 'They'll be expecting me to revive the cooking fires.' She strokes my face, then my head. 'Do what you must to survive! Lie to the priest if you must.' She vanishes into the shadows without looking back at me.

Then I see that the guard is awake and watching both of us.

Run right now! I beg her silently. Don't wait!

The shadows of the barn fill with dark shifting bodies and teeth. In a far corner, a wolf-like shape ripples in the darkness. With her gone, a storm of fear hits me.

Grain baskets, I tell myself.

The shadow wolf moves but comes no closer.

My death, waiting for me.

Lie to the priest, she said.

What lie did she mean? I don't feel that I killed Alice or the hen, but I can't be certain. I'm sure I do not imagine the sense of being invaded by a wolf-like creature.

Sleep is not possible; sleep is death's shadow. For me to die is not possible, but I may die soon. My imagination weighs the dreadful alternatives. Which method of execution hurts the most? Choking at the end of a rope? Or drowning underwater like a wizard? I imagine holding my breath, fighting against breathing in. Then, unable to help it, I inhale the scalding pain of water instead of air.

Or I burn on a pyre: my long fingers catching fire, my nails flaring like candles, fingers turning black and hard like sausages, falling onto the coals, then crumbling to ash. I imagine my fat sizzling, my blood boiling, my body clenched against unimaginable agony.

A rooster crowing in the dark makes my hair stand on end. I stare blankly at a shadowy pair of barn kittens which race stiff-tailed across the floor of my stall and disappear around the raw wood wall. A horse a few stalls away gives a fluttery sigh and shifts its weight. The probable last night of my life is unrolling. I cannot bear it a moment longer, but I must.

The single minor-voiced bell begins to ring. Not for prayers or a meal.

# 4

Grillet and another man drag me from my stall, feet freed but wrists still tied. My legs will not support me. Men and women crowd the barn door or stand just inside. I feel their eyes like knives. A woman screams as I am pulled past her. I turn my head to the sound and think I glimpse a white-faced silent Kat. But I am hauled forward before I can be certain.

She should not be here! Should be running.

Then I see the priest waiting for me at the far end of the barn and forget even Kat. The exorcist. The man who will say what I am and how best to kill me.

I am paralysed for a moment. Back-lit by a flaming torch, the priest stands in front of a small portable altar that looks out of place as if cut from a painting of a church, whether old or new Catholic, and dropped into the barn, complete with white embroidered cloth, two silver candlesticks, and an ornate gilded crucifix. In the air, cedar wood and frankincense mingle incongruously with horse dung, hay and garlic. The new English church resembles the old Papist faith. This priest even wears a floor-length black cassock.

Grillet and the other man drop me at his feet. I look up. He is almost as tall as I am, with a thin face like a knife blade. His eyes burn intensely into mine. I search them for some sign that he sees another human being, but I find only hungry interest and fierce purpose.

His voice reaches out to all his audience. 'You ask me how best to kill this accused murderer. This is not a simple question. First, I must determine the nature of his demon."

"The nature of his demon." He has already decided what I am.

He pauses while the crowd mutters and a recording clerk, sitting on a stool to one side of the altar, scribbles with pen and ink a large black book.

'In examining this apparent youth before witnesses...' He indicates Grillet and the other man who had dragged me there.

"Apparent youth," my mind echoes.

'...I will reach one of several possible conclusions. He may be a pure fiend, terrible to men's eyes, that chooses at will to take the shape of a man in order to carry out its

49

evil work in the human world. These fiends include the devil himself.'

His lean face blazes with fervour. His audience listens in total silence.

'Or he might be a double creature: by day, the demon passes for an ordinary man, but at night it assumes the animal form that always lurks in it, to carry out its bloody deeds under cover of darkness. These double creatures include the werewolf, which you believe this youth to be.

'In both cases – the first case of pure fiend and the second of a double creature who appears to be a man by day – we are at risk when we kill it. The rites and rules of the Church must be carefully followed, or else the devil will return seeking revenge.'

The crowd stirs uneasily.

'Yes, revenge. We must take care.' He looks around the crowd. 'However, this youth may be merely human...'

'No,' Grillet shouts. His shout is followed by murmurs from others in the crowd.

The priest waits until the protests die down. Then, holding up two fingers, he drops the first, his forefinger. 'First of all, he might be a wizard – a mere mortal man, but one who has embraced the devil instead of God as his master. With the devil's help, he can transform himself at will, into a mouse, for example, or a hare or a cat...a wolf, you say in this case...in order to commit his crimes undetected as a man. With the devil's help, he and his female counterparts, witches, can cast evil spells, raise storms, infect the udders of cows or make other mischief. However, because he is merely human, he can be safely hanged, drowned or burnt without reference to Church rules.' The clerk scratches with his pen.

I try to think what being 'merely' human means. It seems no better or worse than being a fiend.

The priest drops the second finger. 'Or else, as a mere human, he may be mad. What doctors call a lycanthrope. In his madness, he believes he is a wolf and murders in the grip of his madness. You may treat him according to human laws.'

I am lost whatever he decides.

Then he closes his fist to hide all his fingers. 'Or he might be entirely innocent.'

I exhale as if he has hit me under the ribs.

'No!' cries Grillet's voice.

'Possessed,' says the priest. 'In that case, he is possessed by an external demon, against his will. He is an innocent man.' The priest looks down at me at his feet. 'When you are possessed in this way, a demon puts you on like a suit of clothes and wears you,' he explains, not unkindly. 'The crime is beyond your wishing or will.'

'Yes, yes!' I murmur.

'If you are that suit of clothes, you are not to be blamed for what a demon does while it wears you. The law does not kill a suit of clothes for the crimes committed by the man who wears it. You do not commit the crime. The possessing demon commits it.'

Have I understood him? That there is a chance I will be found innocent, blameless in spite of Grillet and Brinkley? In spite of my loss of memory and the changes I have sensed in my body?

'Unbind him so I can examine him,' orders the priest.

'No!' Grillet protests again.

'Unbind him! He must stand freely before God.'

An innocent suit of clothes. Not to blame. The demon wearing me killed Alice. I did not kill Alice Brinkley even if my physical hands and teeth tore her apart… my hands and teeth. The thought makes me queasy but not as terrified as execution. I see a way out. And Kat can believe what she likes.

I hold up my bound hands. Grillet unties them, eyes averted.

I set my right foot on the floor, try to straighten my leg. I cannot stand upright. The foot feels like a block of wood, will not take my weight. I fall to my hands and knees and pant with the effort, shoulders heaving. The blood burns back into my legs. My feet throb.

The priest watches me struggle. 'He has difficulty standing erect like an innocent man,' he dictates.

The clerk writes in his book

I must seem human. Human and possessed. Innocent.

I try again. Place my foot, straighten the leg, stagger, catch myself. Stamp my foot. Though still bent, my right leg holds. Then my left leg takes my weight. I am standing.

The priest's fingers then explore my body inch by inch: behind my ears, my hands, in my armpits, my back, my belly, working downward. A fine dark fuzz covers part of my arms and legs. I feel his fingers hesitate on them.

How much smooth skin is needed to be human? I wonder.

The man's fingers return to the bottom of my back. 'There is a wolf patch at the base of his spine.' he says thoughtfully. 'I also find dark hair on the joints of his fingers and toes.'

The clerk writes.

'However, he has no moles, extra nipples or witch marks to indicate beyond doubt that he is a devil or demon.'

I wait for the verdict, scarcely able to breathe.

'The evidence, therefore, is so far inconclusive.' The priest turns to the altar, seizes the crucifix and holds it above my head with both hands. 'Kneel and fix your eyes on our Saviour's face!'

What would an innocent suit of clothes do now? I hesitate.

A fist yanks me back onto my knees by my hair. Grillet's voice breathes in my ear. I feel his hot breath but do not understand his words. The bright globe of his head contracts in the jumping torchlight behind the priest, then swells again.

Voices begin to boom around the walls. The fist holds my hair too tightly for me to move. I squeeze my eyes shut against the light.

'Does the sight of our Holy Saviour offend you'?' asks the priest's voice, distant and faint.

The leaping flames fill my head. Snap, snap, snap...

'You'll never look!' breathes an intense voice in my ear. 'The devil can't abide a holy sight.'

Shadow beasts writhe deep in my memory.

Snap, snap, snap...

I start to fall into a cold, dark current, deeper and deeper into the black icy water of a bottomless lake. My beast is coming.

*Not now!* I struggle to hold it off.

The fist lets go of my hair. A belch of terror rises from my stomach and jams against the underside of my vocal chords. Terror and foreboding flood through me. The floor beneath me, the air around me, dissolve and swirl like oil on water.

I hold on to the present world with all my will.

The air and floor slowly turn solid again. The beast retreats a little, not gone but farther away. Biding its time. I fall forward onto hands and knees, exhausted by the struggle.

'Can you look at the crucifix?' repeats the priest with a hint of impatience. 'Or do you turn away?'

I lift my head and clamp heavy eyes uncertainly onto the pink painted face under a crown of painted thorns.

'I can look...'

It is the right choice.

The priest turns to the two witnesses. 'Will you both testify that he is not repulsed by this holy sight?' They nod, wide-eyed, even Grillet.

Whatever the truth may be, I must be found an innocent suit of clothes. 'Father, I know I am possessed..!'

'That is for me to say. The devil in you lies by its nature.' He replaces the crucifix on the altar. Then he turns to me again. 'Do you ever feel melancholy?'

How could I not? 'Yes.'

'Or feel constricted or stifled?'

The squeezing fist.

'Yes,' I whisper.

The priest nods. 'Or as if a sort of ball ascended into the gullet?'

The rising bubble of horror I have just felt.

'Yes. Yes.'

'And when you pass wind from your gut, does it ever smell of sulphur?'

Unable to speak, I can only nod.

'And feel a lethargy, as if you did not wish to live?

I nod twice again. Yes. Yes.

'And are you ever seized by fear and terror?'

He is describing my experience exactly. I nod once more.

The priest puts his hands on my shoulders and lifts his face to the crowd. 'The weight of evidence tells me that this youth is not a devil but human. Furthermore, he is not a wizard who can cast evil spells on your cattle or crops, or call down floods and freezing snow. Nor is he mad. I find him to be possessed, and his possessing demon is the culprit. This youth is both human and innocent of killing Alice Brinkley or the hen. The devil in him killed them, not he.'

'So what are we supposed to do about my hen? demands Grillet.

'And my Alice is still dead!' shouts Brinkley from the crowd.

Tears of relief blur my eyes as I gaze up at the priest. I am an innocent suit of clothes after all.

'But the possessing demon still remains in him and might strike again,' he warns.

'Then I beg you, father, cast it out!' I cry. If he can. Demon or not, there is something there. I do not have to lie to him.

Then I have a chilling thought. A possessing demon will surely fight being torn out of a comfortable suit of clothes. It will resist viciously, sinking claws into the heart and guts to hold on.

'A possessing demon will not yield easily,' the priest warns. 'It will feel the full terror of God's wrath.'

But I must be rid of my wolf...or whatever it is! I nod. 'Proceed.'

'Prepare to have your heart wrenched out.'


The priest banishes the watching crowd lest the exorcised demon jump from me into one of them. He blesses Grillet and the other witnessing farmer to protect them against the same possibility. Without warning, he makes the sign of the Cross and flings wide his arms. 'You do not alarm me, demon!' he bellows to the roof of the barn. 'In man, in lion, in fish, you are just the same!'

We wait.

Nothing shouts back.

The stillness grows.

No devil howls with rage at being challenged.

The priest lays one end of his purple silk stole across my shoulder as a bridge between our souls. I brace on both knees. 'I beg God's grace for this exorcism against the wicked dragon,' he says more quietly. 'I exorcise thee, most vile spirit. Go out! Tarry not!'

Again, silence.

No demonic claws hook tightly into my guts. If it is really there inside me, the demon – my wolf – is ignoring the priest's invitation to leave.

Please! I beg it silently. Whatever you are! You 've already changed my life! Go before you kill me! I throw my head back, throat open, holding the gate wide for it to go.

'You lean mangy sow beast, swollen toad, may God set a nail in your skull!' shouts the priest.

I feel nothing in my throat or gut.

But if I am to be judged innocent, my demon must be seen to leave. Therefore...My brain grinds sluggishly...I must pretend. Shout and writhe, clutch my belly as if it was going, even if I feel nothing.

Was this what Kat meant by 'lie to the priest'?

He slaps my face.

# 5

'It needs fiercer persuasion. We must make your body an unwelcoming home from which the demon will choose to flee.' He slaps me again.

Head spinning, I feel myself lifted and laid belly down on a table. My head overhangs one end. Below my head burns a smoking brazier of coals. The rising smoke clogs my lungs. If I do not act now, I will be past pretending, whether my demon has left or not.

I howl in what I hope is a demonic voice. 'I go!' I choke on the smoke from the brazier and begin to cough violently. 'I go,' I whisper between coughs.

'He lies!' shouts Grillet's voice. 'The demon is still in him!'

'I submit!' I growl. 'I depart...'

The first blow of a whip hits me across the shoulders. Too shocked to think any longer how I should act, I try to struggle up from the table, but hands hold me down.

Green branches are thrown onto the coals in the brazier. Thick black smoke billows up. A cloth dropped over my head directs the smoke into my face. I hold my breath.

I drown in smoke. Must inhale. The smoke burns my lungs. I choke. My eyes stream.

'Thou liest, vile toad, thou deceiving dragon!'

A second whip lash burns into my back.

'For thee and thy fallen angels is prepared the unquenchable fire,' I hear him faintly. More green wood... herbs thicken the smoke further. Consciousness begins to come and go.

'Yield to the God...beats thee with divine scourges...'

Lungs on fire. My back flames with pain. The inside of my head throbs red. Can't breathe. Air as black and solid as hot mud.

'You... kill me,' I manage to gasp.

'Better to kill the mortal body than lose the immortal soul.' The voice is distant.

Smoke chars the linings of my nostrils and seeps into the shafts of my hair. My eyeballs turn into smoke-filled globes.

'Even if the demon kills you from spite as it flees,' says the mosquito hum of the distant voice, 'you can rejoice that your soul will live!'

'I can prove that the demon is still in him...' Someone pulls away the cloth trapping the smoke.

'No! Master Grillet! Stand back!' the distant voice shouts. 'The demon might shift!'

Grillet thrusts a torch into my face. 'Look how he still turns away. The demon turns from light!'

I force myself to look at the light.

Everything begins to jump and judder in the flames of the torch: the priest, the little altar beyond him, the barn itself. The belch of terror rises from my stomach again, Again, it jams against the underside of my vocal chords. The giant fist begins to tighten again around my chest. The beast comes into sight...closer. This time, I can't fight.

*I brush against him.*

Beast, you will kill me if you come now!

The barn, the floor beneath my knees, the air around me... swirls again like oil on water. I become part of the clamour around me. This time, I can't fight the fall into darkness.

*I climb onto his shoulder.*

The tightening fist presses the beast into my head. A wolf grows like coral into the spaces in my bones. Its muscles lap around mine and worm through the fibres of my being like fungus under tree bark.

The fist squeezes my chest and closes my throat so that only a thread of air gets through. A nail of pain drives through the dull ache in my skull.

The thread of air grows thinner.

I feel the muscles of my face and scalp shift. I feel my limbs lengthen. My ears pull back on my skull. The beast reshapes me in its own image. The fist loosens to make room for the beast room inside me. All sounds grow sharp edges.

The bubble of horror spreads up into my throat.

I'm…

I…

But I have no words.

*I am the wolf.*


*A scream pierces my skull. The leaping flames seem to have set others alight.*

*Fire! Run!*

*Suddenly, the hands that hold me loosen.*

*The stench of burning and of human fear clogs my nostrils. Blind with terror, I struggle up from the table, knock aside warm bodies and their clouds of foetid sweat, bolt, lashed by shouts and screams, jarred by the blast of a musket. Sharp fragments sting my shoulder.*

*A huge, bright light leaps and twists across the stable yard. The smell of burning hay fills my head. Shouts and screams pound at me. I smell human terror all around me. I turn and plunge towards the refuge of darkness.*

*In the flickering light, I bump into barrels, climb onto a hay cart, claw my way over the barnyard wall. Beyond the wall, I sniff the darkness. Smell directs me away from terror towards the clean peaceful scents of darkness and water. I jump a water-filled ditch. Silky fur slides over my muscles, dulling their pain.*

*Behind me, flames jump against the night sky. Even from here, where I stop and crouch to listen, I can hear the crackling. A girl's voice calls in the darkness.*

I pause uncertainly. I can't reply, even if I want to. I can think of words, but something has cut the string between thought and tongue.

'Rafe?'

Here in the darkness, the beast begins to leave me. But I still can't answer.

'Don't fear. It's your friend, Kat.' Her shape draws closer. 'Don't you know me?'

Kat.

My teeth begin to clatter. I'm coming back. Coming back. I wrap my arms around myself to hold it all together. A fragile shell around ebbing pandemonium.

My eyelids droop. The beast has stolen all my strength.

'Rafe? Can you understand me?

She steps closer.

I scramble away from her into the shadows of a hedgerow.

'Rafe.' She speaks calmly and firmly. 'I'm trying to make you safe. Do you understand me?' She holds out her hand.

Head raised, I test the air to be certain she is alone.

Safe with Kat.

I lie down on the ground under the hedge, helpless to remain on my feet a moment longer. I drop my head onto my folded arms.

Safe.

Sleep floods into the hollow space left behind by the beast.

'You can't sleep yet!' She hauls roughly at my arm. 'Too close to the farm. They're still fighting the fire, but once they stop trying to save the hay barn, they'll come after you with the dogs,'

'Sleep,' I protest.

'Sleep later! You must escape now!' She tries to pull me up by the shoulders. 'You're too broad for me to get a good grip. Please stand up! I don't want to hurt you, but I won't let you stay here!'

She takes a deep breath and pushes her hands under my armpits. I feel her fingers in the damp silky hair under my arms. The hair on her head tickles my face and a smoky smell fills my nostrils. She heaves at me again.

This time, I let her pull me to my feet, my weight pressed against her side. She slings my arm across her shoulders. Her cheek presses against the warm ridges of my right ear.

As if I was embracing her, I think groggily. I feel her hand move lower on my back, searching for unbroken skin.

'Good.' She soothes me like a dog. 'Now, walk with me. This way.' My hip bumps against hers.

'It's fortunate that I'm so tall and strong,' she says. 'Or I'd have to leave you.'

My head droops forward, but my legs keep moving. She sees me look back.

Flames leap into the night sky, brighter and hotter than the moonlight. 'The hay barn,' she says shortly. 'Just a little farther...' She stops to readjust my weight. 'They may already be giving your scent to the dogs.'

Two startled sheep bolt bleating from the shadows of the hedgerow just ahead of us. She curses under her breath. 'Why not just shout, "Here they are! Here they are!"'

She drags me faster across the field. More sheep mill and bleat. Over a small ditch... clumsily, slip into the water, wet feet. Back up into another field. No sheep.

'Down here...' She helps me down four steep, slippery wooden steps in the bank of a large water-filled drainage canal and half-drops me into a dinghy moored to a post.

I curl up in the bottom of the boat, safe at last.

'Rafe!'

She is shaking me. 'Not yet! Dear God, wake up! Help shove us free!'

I push up onto my hands, then shove at the bank as she directs. Backlit by the moonlight, her silhouette poises seated in the middle of the boat, an oar in each hand, listening. I gaze at the astonishing sight of Kat in the boat with me.

We are in a small rowing dinghy, the fish-man's, by the smell of it. My head aches and I feel dazed, a burnt-out shell. My eyes still weep from the smoke. But the wolfish beast has gone. A fit of coughing rips at my muscles.

'Hush!' she says. '...if you can.'

I try to stop coughing. Between bouts of silent gasps, I hear ducks muttering in the reeds. Then dogs begin to bark in the distance. I lift my head to listen.

She dips the oars in the dark water and heaves. 'We're still too close.'

The suppressed coughing finally eases. 'Where should we go?' I croak. I have no idea where I am, beyond England itself.

'Find a large town, harder for the dogs to follow you. With luck, you can lose yourself among all the people.'

I start to say, I can't lose myself as I am, but I don't want to call attention to my nakedness.

As if I have spoken, she reaches behind her and tosses me a roughly-tied bundle of clothes. 'Snatched these from the washhouse in too much haste to make fine judgements about fit.' She looks over her shoulder at where she is rowing. Against the current, away from the sea. 'But better than wandering around as bare as the day you were born.'

The underdrawers and breeches come to my knee rather than my calf and are huge around the waist but they cover me. I wince as I pull on the pale linen shirt. It is short in the sleeve but loose enough to hang away from the two whip stripes on my back.

'Owner of the breeches must be short and fat. I hope these aren't his only ones.' She rows another stroke. 'Did your demon come during the exorcism?'

My smoke-burnt lungs refuse to take a deep breath. 'Yes.'

She rows a few more strokes. 'Therefore, I have seen you when you were visited by your beast?'

I nod. Easier than speaking.

'I will swear on whatever you like that you did not transform in any way. You behaved strangely, I admit.

Something serious ails you, but you did not turn into a wolf.'

'I felt it come. Felt it change me. You could not have seen clearly.'

'I saw well enough!' She gives a sharp pull on the oars and the boat surges forward in the black water.

I tie the shirt in silence. The home-spun, sleeveless wool doublet she has stolen is tight across my shoulders, but I can keep up the over-large knee-length breeches by tying them to a series of metal-tipped laces hanging from the doublet.

'No shoes or stockings, I fear. But there's a cap near where you're sitting.' The boat surges ahead again.

I reach down, feel around and find an apprentice's cap, a soft, flat, dark wool bun with a wide stiff brim.

When dressed, I force my muscles to hold me straight in the boat. In spite of pain in back and lungs, I feel fully human for the first time since being captured. My pleasure is short-lived.

She turns the boat towards the bank and ships the oars. The boat rocks as she stands to climb out. 'You'll have to row now. Keep going upstream. You're headed for Cambridge.'

'Kat...' I seize her skirt.

She bends down so that our faces are close in the dark. 'Yes?' she whispers.

'Did you set the hay barn alight?'

'They were killing you!' Her fierce breath stirs the cool night air.

My brain struggles to take in the thought that this amazing girl, Kat, torched the hay barn to save me. Whatever she believes, she has not left me to die. I want to throw my arms around her and hold her tightly so that she can't leave.

'You can't go back either!' I say. 'You're in just as much danger. Weren't you seen coming after me? The dogs must have your scent too.' I release her skirt and grab her hands. They are cold and wet. 'I know it's dangerous to be with me.'

'Don't fear.' In the dark, I do not see the look she undoubtedly gives me. 'I'll never go back there! To Master Grillet and his wandering hands! And his pleasure in beating me the way he did a runaway groom. I'll make my own way. I know how to survive.'

I imagine her shape blending into the shadowy lances of the reeds, the brush of her skirts against them sucked up by the breath of the night. I feel tiny and insignificant in the open flatness of the land under the great dark bowl of the sky. Even now, before she has left me, the night feels huge and frightening.

'Come with me.'

She yanks her hands free. 'As what? Your serving maid?'

'Serving maid? Why do you say that?' I dare not say what I truly hope. 'As a...whatever you like. I don't know...But please come.'

There is a long silence.

'You don't know what you're saying. When your body has recovered, you'll think differently. I'm a foundling, remember? Spawn of the devil, a lowly scullery maid.'

'I'm an Amsterdam street-rat, who may be a werewolf as well.'

'You don't know the whole of it yet!' She hesitates. Then the dinghy rocks as she resettles and unships the oars again. 'I'll row a little longer. Get you away from here!'

She is silent for several strokes. She dips her oars, pulls them through the water, dips them again. 'I'm most likely the bastard of some light-heeled trull who couldn't even name the father of her babe.'

I hear slight defiance in her words.

'Until I left London, I used the foundling hospital uniform and my blue eyes and blonde curls to play the innocent while I cut purses – which I was rather good at, I may add.' Her dark shape pats its pocket. 'I still have my little knife.'

A test for me. She does not say, 'What do you think of that? But I hear the words floating in the air.

'And I'm a Dutch street rat who sang for whores in brothels. I don't need a serving maid. I need a companion who knows this strange country and its ways. Who doesn't mind the risk of being with a possible werewolf.'

She rows a few more strokes. I can almost hear her thinking.

'Werewolf or not, you're also an English gentleman. You've come to England to become a gentleman...after you get rid of your wolf... have you not?' Her cool voice reminds me of her strangeness in the barn.

'Is reclaiming the family estate a difficulty?' I ask.

'You may not think so now, but it will become one if you can do it. Trust me.'

'I don't feel like a gentleman,' I protest. 'It's just a part I must learn to play here in England - as far as the wolf, which you insist I don't turn into, will let me. If you can play both innocent and thief, why can't I play a part as well?'

Her shadow shrugs.

We surge upstream in silence for a while.

'Are we still headed for Cambridge?' I ask, testing the 'we'.

''It's the nearest large town.' She does not respond to my 'we'. 'The market town of Grillet's estate... or at least the only one I've been to.' She rests a moment, breathing hard and stretching her back. 'And there's a university there. Superstition and religion have tried to kill you. Perhaps you should try Cambridge's learned doctors and their famous Reason.' She begins to pull at the oars again. 'You might listen to them, if you won't listen to me.'

I sink back, happier than I can remember, which is not very long, I admit.  But I am happy, nevertheless.

She lifts her head. 'I can hear dogs! They've loosed the dogs after us.'

I've heard the dogs already, baying in the distance.

Her shape gives small grunts of effort as she propels us rapidly through the dark water. The dogs fade in the distance. The burning hay barn becomes a faint orange glow on the horizon. Lulled by the surges of the dinghy, I feel less real than the occasional splash or wet plop of an unseen water bird or rat. High veils of pale cloud seem more solid than my body. At last, I sleep.

# 6

I wake abruptly. The dogs sound closer again. We are drifting the wrong way. Back the way we came.

Kat slumps over the oars.

'Kat!' I whisper.

She stirs and begins to row furiously back up-current, not fully awake.

In the wildly rocking dinghy, I ease her drowsy body into my place in the bottom of the boat, ignoring her protests. I take the oars and slide the blades into the black water. The two whip cuts on my back sting, but the act of rowing is familiar.

I suddenly fill with the memory of rowing on the Amsterdam canals. Cramped muscles stretch and loosen. I dip and haul, dip and haul, my long legs pump, finding my rhythm, fast and hard, away from the dogs, towards Cambridge.

The more tolerant England with its new Scottish king, James who took the English throne after the death of the terrifying Virgin Elizabeth, might accept me as a Catholic refugee from the Continent back to reclaim my heritage as an Englishman. But, I am certain that, however tolerant it is now, England will never offer safety to the demon wolf, for want of a better description, that I know lurks inside me, as unpredictable and terrifying to me as to other people. I listen to Kat's gentle breathing. I will not be safe anywhere on earth while the wolf is in me, and she will not be safe with me. If I don't hurt her, other people will.

Cam...bridge. Cam...bridge. Water splashes from my oars. Even Amsterdam has heard of Cambridge. A whore's client in a musico once said that Cambridge scholars are at ease with knowledge that most men are too ignorant even to wonder about. He was drunk but seemed to know what he was talking about. 'They know,' he had said, waving his arms, 'about the structure of the heavens, the mathematical dance of the stars, how to brew potent medicines, the anatomy of dogs and angels.'

For a number of strokes, I consider the last.

My hands blister. The blisters break. Clouds cover and uncover the moon. The sound of baying dogs has faded behind us. I will take up Kat's suggestion of trying to find a helpful scholar in Cambridge. At this point, I will try anything to remove my wolf.

I must also tell her that we must part, for a time at least, until my wolf is gone, however much we may want to stay together.

The sky is just beginning to turn slate grey with false dawn. Kat suddenly wakes. 'We should be going that way! More or less.' She points in sleepy panic away from the river to the west. Sitting in the bottom of the dinghy where I have carefully laid her, she flexes her fingers and rotates her shoulders painfully. 'Anyway, by now they've surely missed the dinghy and be looking for two people in a boat.'

I need her to get me to Cambridge. She'll be as safe with me there as anywhere, if we don't, while getting there, meet an early shepherd or fish-man, and if I don't transform again. I decide not to speak yet.

At the next shallow tributary flowing from the left, we put rocks into the dinghy and sink it with the oars wedged in the bottom. Then Kat hoicks up her skirt and petticoat and we plough up the tributary through water that grows shallower the further we wade upstream. When the stream dwindles to a trickle, we climb the shallow bank and battle through brambles.

We stop together without saying a word. Beyond a field of drowsing cattle, a dry ditch is about five feet deep and clear of nettles and bramble.

'Rest...just for a moment.' Kat slides down into the ditch and I jump after her. She curls up in her shawl.

'I've been wanting to ask - it *is* spring?' I say sleepily. She nods, already half-asleep.

The next I know, the horizon bleeds pink light, flushing the sky with the warning of a wet day. I stretch cautiously. 'Rested too long.' But my head feels better. And, though I must part from her soon, Kat has not yet deserted me.

'You haven't eaten me yet.' She brushes shadowy leaves and grass from her clothes. 'Not far to go now.' She digs in her skirt for a grubby linen handkerchief and spits on it. 'Sit down. That dried blood in your hair may draw the wrong kind of attention.'

I sit obediently cross-legged on the base of the ditch. She leans close to peer and dabs intently at my left temple. I flinch but do not pull away. I close my eyes. Otherwise, I will stare at her rounded bosom so near my face. I smell the sweat of the night's rowing on both of us, the freshness of the open air and the coppery tang of my blood. Musty earth and sharp green broken grass from the ditch. Under it all, I smell her body.

'I thought you'd left me in the barn.'

She dabs silently at my head. 'I almost did,' she says at last. She dabs a little more. 'There are gulfs between people, not just between werewolf and human.' She spits on the handkerchief again. 'But I couldn't let them kill you, no matter what you are.' Her hands are gentler than her voice. 'Someone hit you hard!'

I suddenly remember. 'Footpads!' I remember watching three men approach me on the road, already alert to a bad feeling in my gut. I exchanged polite greetings, had just passed them. Then they attacked me from behind. I should have been watching them. I feel the fight in my muscles. I feel the blow on my head and their tugging at me.

I can't remember after that. 'They must have taken my purse and my clothes...And my lute!' My arms embrace its ghost.

I suddenly see its painted wooden lute case, lying on my narrow bunk on the tossing ship from Amsterdam to England.

Sweet-voiced, made of pear wood and maple, with a long, beautiful ebony neck.' My left hand slides over invisible frets. My right hand seeks the strings. 'I think I meant to sing my way to that "home" in Lincolnshire.'

For a moment, joy fills me, the joy of effortlessly doing what I most love – singing. For money, for whores and drinkers in musicos …in inns...it does not matter where. 'I miss it.' I say. And not just for the joy. 'I earned my crossing to England by playing and singing for the sailors. Even though my stomach churned!'

'That's better.' Kat tucks the handkerchief back into her skirts.

I stand and look down at her. For a moment, I imagine the future with her. But it is impossible. I am still wanted for murder, or my demon wolf is. I'm as dangerous as I ever was. The priest gave me hope but failed to exorcise the wolf. I must get rid of it or else think no further.

The rising sun suddenly spills across the flat fields and touches distant buildings. Against black shadows carved out by the early light, they glow as if lit by a fire.

'Cambridge?' I ask.

The road is already busy with farmers and their wives with black and white pigs being herded, with geese, brown hens' eggs, vivid green water cress and pale green over-wintered cabbages. I keep my head down as I walk. My height, my ill-fitting clothes and filthy bare feet seem to be shouting my guilt. I start to say that we must part. But I can't get the words out.

She studies the morning crowds massing to go through a town gate. 'Your scholar should be wearing some kind of fine black robe, not like these in their straw hats and brown homespun,' she mutters. 'You go look for him.'

'And you?' Perhaps she intends to say farewell, too. But we are suddenly in a current of people passing through the gate. I narrowly miss stepping on a goose. Once we get inside the gate, she measures my bare feet with her eyes.

'Shoes or boots might confuse the dogs. I'll have a sniff around for some. And who knows what else?' She grins. 'If neither of us is arrested, I'll meet you at midday around that next corner in the Market Place.' She flashes me a glimpse of a little knife on a ring on her middle finger. 'My cuttle-bung. For cutting purses.' She seems to saunters away but moves too fast into a press of merchants with baskets of eggs and cabbages for me to stop her.

I do need shoes, I reason. Taking the shoes, I can see her once more. See her once more, touch her. I gaze after her but can't see where she has gone.

Now for that scholar. But inside the city gate, as outside, no one wears black scholars robes or looks notably wise. I imagine walking up to a stranger: 'How do you? Are you a scholar? May I beg your help? I'm a werewolf.' Smiling in derision, I round the corner to where Kat said she would meet me at the midday bell – an open square set with market stalls.

On my right, a man is nailing a placard to a post. A growing crowd clusters around him. I edge closer and peer over a woman's shoulder. 'BEWARE SAVAGE AND BLOODY ACTS.' The placard is illustrated with a woodcut: a half-clothed man with a wolf's head gnaws a severed, booted human leg.

A man who has learned his letters reads aloud to a man who has not. 'A creature possessed by the devil and using the name "Rafe Seabright"…'

I glance around the crowd.

'…handsome of face… black hair and of more than usual height…'

I slouch to reduce my height.

'…black brows…distinctive amber eyes… ' reads the man, 'without warning takes on the fiendish shape of a wolf…did kill and eat a five-year-old girl named…'

The farmers or the priest. It came to the same thing – suit of clothes or not, I had killed Alice Brinkley.

'Oh, Sweet Lord, a child-killer!' a woman near me exclaims. 'One moment it's a man, the next a monster. It might be any of us here.' She gazes uneasily at the people around her. 'How does one knows it?'

'The placard says you should watch out for a tall, handsome man. Don't you always?' says the short round man beside her.

I pull my cap low to hide my distinctive amber eyes. I slouch further. The chase for me has already reached Cambridge.

'REWARD!' reads the man who has learned his letters. 'For information leading to capture or for its head and paws…' My head, my hands.

I ease back out of the crowd.

Get out of the city!

84

But dogs might be heading this way across the fields at the very moment.

A hand grabs my sleeve. I yank free in terror.

Kat takes my arm again more firmly. 'It's too late for scholars. We've got to get out of Cambridge. Both of us. Over there to our right...by the clay pipe seller. Listen!'

A ballad seller stands on a barrel. His fine tenor soars above the gathered heads of a small crowd.

*May God protect the innocent child*
*Who sweetly plays while the werewolf wild*
*With lantern eyes and bloodied teeth*
*Stalks for prey across the heath...*

When he finishes singing, he begins to sell copies. Eager hands reach and hand him coins.

The failure of the demon to leave me outweighs the priest's verdict of 'innocent suit of clothes'. As long as my wolf is still in me, I am dangerous.

I let Kat lead me down an alley but after a few strides, I pull free of her grip. 'You must leave me now. You'll be safer. Go!' The words tumble out without thought in spite of my rehearsing.

She turns back to look for pursuers. 'Giving up?

'Nowhere is safe for you with me. I have to tear out my wolf.'

Two young men cross our alley in a bigger street ahead, carrying papers and books. They wear black scholars' gowns.

'There! They may lead...' I say desperately. 'Get rid of the wolf, clear myself of Alice's death. Only then...'

Awkward at this sudden goodbye, I turn from her and follow the two young men.

After several paces, Kat speaks behind me. 'Couldn't find any shoes or boots. Shoemakers too watchful.'

'Please leave me,' I beg. I try to ignore her.

I must not lose the young men. They look like vicars but talk of mathematics and women. From what I can hear, they are not entirely reasonable about women but seem at ease with mathematics. Kat still follows me.

The young men lead into a maze of streets and passages where shops and market stalls become high brick walls and important-looking gates. The young men disappear through one of the gates. When I try to follow them, a gatekeeper blocks my way. 'We don't want your sort in here! Clear off!'

I duck behind a second group of young men in black robes standing outside a second gate, talking in excitement.

'I don't belong here for certain,' mutters Kat. She pulls on my arm. 'Neither of us looks like we belong.'

I put out a hand. I want to hear what the second group of young men are saying.

'You don't dare come, because you might be proved wrong!' says one young man in a tight voice. Chest puffed out, he eyes another young man in black robes like cockerel squaring up to fight.

Four other youths in black nudge each other in anticipation.

'If you're determined to stay,' Kat murmurs under her breath, 'At least we can eat. I'll see what food I can filch. And find a purse or two ripe for nipping. You'll need both, whatever you decide to do. Find me here.'

'Wait!' But she is already strolling away down the cobbled lane. I almost follow her, then turn back to the young men.

The first continues in a tight voice. '...The doctor's demonstration of anatomy this afternoon will prove you – and your so-called "authorities" – completely wrong!'

'Heretic!' the second young man shouts, his face red with fury. 'God made a perfect Universe. How dare you or your "doctor" question His Work by presuming to examine it for yourself!'

The other four nod, agreeing with him. I am interested, however, in the first young man, the questioning heretic who backs this doctor of anatomy who observes for himself.

The second man pokes a finger in the chest of the heretic. 'How dare you, a mere student, imagine that you're wiser than the Ancient Greek and Latin authorities who have described this perfect Universe?'

'I may not be wiser,' the first youth retorts. He squints down at the prodding finger. 'But I'm far more observant. And my authority is very much alive – he's come from Padua to challenge your ancient – and very dead – so-called authorities, including Galen, on human anatomy. Not only is he very much alive, but he teaches in the very latest, modern, observational way. Not the ancient hearsay filled with error that you're so happy to swallow blindly with your eyes squeezed tightly shut.'

Alive. Observant. Modern. An expert in Anatomy. I may have found possible help...or least advice...if I can get to this doctor from Padua.

'I dare all of you to risk losing your ignorance.' The first youth stares in challenge at the other five. 'Come listen to the doctor from Padua demonstrate today in the theatre of anatomy.' He points at the closed gate outside which we stand. 'He has a fresh human corpse, newly executed at dawn this morning. And new information for his audience. Everyone wants to hear him.' He gestures around him at the growing crowd.

I want to hear him. My own universe has recently proved to be far from perfect.

The closed gate opens. The men gathered in the street pour thorough, men in black joined by men in damask coats and plumed hats. One of the latter balances a monkey on his shoulder. My young men are sucked in, still arguing. I follow the crowd and join the man with the monkey. I smile and nod as if I agree with something he is saying and squeeze through, praying that no one will notice my dirty bare feet.

The crowd carries me across a courtyard into a building on the far side and up a narrow wooden staircase. Going up the stairs, my nose is pressed against a pair of blue, silk-clad male shoulder blades that smell of musk and rosewater. I spy a single woman a few stairs up from me and wonder what she is doing here. The man with the monkey laughs with another man wearing red silk and a white-plumed hat. They don't feel like scholars at all.

I've come to the wrong place, I think. This is a crowd come to see theatre or a travelling menagerie. But I am wedged in place by bodies, unable to turn back down the narrow stairs.

Then the crowd expands through double doors at the top of the stairs. I look around curiously and find myself on the highest of ascending tiers of a small wooden amphitheatre built in a horseshoe. Large windows in the roof let in morning light. Through bobbing hat plumes and bright silk arms raised in greeting, I see reassuring black robes and the sheer muslin collars of scholars near the front, on the bottom two tiers. My six young men from the street stand on the second tier to my right. The woman seems to be an artist; she sets out her charcoal and paper right at the front. I am temporarily as safe here in the crowd as anywhere. And the doctor from Padua might know what to do about my wolf, in spite of my reservations. I sidle to a free space at the waist-high railing which runs along the front edge of each tier and look down.

A short set of wooden stairs leads from each end of the wooden horseshoe down to a flat semi-circular floor. On the floor squats a wooden table, as scrubbed and purposeful as if in a kitchen, with a smaller table standing near it. A large box of sawdust is tucked under it. Through the musk and civet perfuming the air, I smell stale blood.

'Even the greatest scholars come to hear him. Look!' The young man beside me stares happily down through the sea of plumes. He wears a soft green velvet cap, a single pearl earring and a cape slung over one shoulder. 'Do you come to hear his heretical raging, too?' he asks. His dog sniffs at my legs.

My attention is frozen on the dog. 'Forgive me...'

The young man takes a closer look at me and moves to a lower tier, calling his dog. After a final sniff, it goes. Then my attention is distracted from the dog.

A man in blue livery enters through a small door in the bottom tier carrying a linen cloth. Everyone watches silently as he unfolds the cloth. He spreads it over the smaller table. He leaves by the same small door in the bottom tier. The crowd murmurs.

After a few moments, he enters again carrying a polished brown wooden chest. The crowd jumps when he drops the chest with a metallic clatter – and far too much relish – on the cloth-covered smaller table. He leaves. The crowd falls silent again.

His blue-clad rump bumps open the small door. He enters backwards; he carries the head of a plain wood coffin; a second servant follows at the foot. They drop it with a thud beside the large scrubbed table.

I hear the spectators breathing and the sighing of their clothes. A boot sole squeaks. Then someone murmurs, answered by a muted laugh.

My pulse beats in my throat. At the same time, I am aware that the doctor from Padua is playing his audience as well as any Amsterdam fairground flimflammer.

Then the crowd stirs on the lowest tier. The doctor himself enters through the same small door as the coffin. He wears re-assuring black scholar's robes. A young woman as tall as he and also in black, follows him. A few people applaud. Two scholars step forward to greet him, but I see several other scholars cross their arms as if to say, 'Convince me!'

The doctor greets those on the front tier, smiling and smiling. He is not what I expected of a wise man who observes for himself and refuses to accept the Ancients blindly. He is not as I imagined: dark and saturnine, all dignity and a grey beard, perhaps with a noble hooked nose and eyes that burned like those of the priest. Instead, made more noticeable by the dignity of the scholars surrounding him, he has the face of a raddled cherub with pillowed, plump cheeks and smiling pink lips. He appears round and soft under his robes. It is hard to tell how old he is. And those smiles! And he waves his arms too much as he speaks.

What am I doing here? I think again. Pinning my life on a clown like that? From what I can see, his audience seems to be divided between avid interest in what he is going to say and what I think.

The tall young woman in black opens the chest and takes out a mallet, a saw, a chisel, tongs, and several knives. She sets them on the small table. Her hands are strong and pale. Hair the colour of winter sunlight escapes from under her white linen cap. She has an air of tranquil authority that her master – or whatever he is – lacks.

My neighbours talk about her under their breath.

'...his assistant – they say.'

'And who knows what else besides? You know the Italians...'

She places the last knife at the end of a graduated row, folds her hands and looks at the doctor. I am trying to decide what to make of her when the doctor speaks.

'Welcome brothers in presumption.' His voice is loud, clear and oiled by self-satisfaction. 'If you brought a closed mind with you, please leave at once.' He scans the tiers. 'No marching feet? No one afraid of heresy? A departure from the accepted truth? I applaud you, for the only true heresy is ignorance.' His eyes assess his audience. He smiles. The little pillows of his cheeks gleam.

A mutter comes from the tier below mine, but no one leaves his place.

'God the great Craftsman made a perfect universe in the beginning, at Creation,' intones the doctor. '"Of course!" I hear you mutter to each other. "What a dull fellow this Italian is. We know that! No heresy here. We've known that for centuries."'

He swings his gaze from one end of the tiers to the other. I imagine that his eyes hesitate on me before moving on.

'But why did He do this? That is the unanswered question. Was it merely for his Own pleasure? It's the old question, and no one has answered it – yet. Until today.' The doctor holds up a modest, disclaiming hand. 'Today, I will dare to give His reason. I will dare speak for God.'

I have to admit that the man is a compelling speaker.

'"Would He be so selfish, to think only of His own pleasure?" I ask. "No!" I say. "God created this perfect universe as a challenge to man's wit."' The doctor's dark eyes definitely meet mine.

I stiffen. Why has he singled me out among so many?

'Some scholars say that we are tampering with Divine Will if we do not accept the so-called "truth" that has been handed down unthinkingly to us for generations. It is called "heresy" whether we examine the generational organs of a frog or Henry, freshly hanged this morning...' He gestures at the coffin.

'He must have slipped the executioner something...not that easy...' a neighbour murmurs.

The doctor peers into eyes, gathering up his listeners. 'I say – I repeat, "I say" – that our so-called "heretical" prying is intended by God. Did He not create man in His image and set alight in us the fire which some call "soul", but I call "mind". Did He not set alight that questing force that distinguishes us from beasts and sets us as master over animals and the vegetable state?' In his passion, he thumps the coffin with his fist.

His words snag at my thoughts like a half-swallowed hook. I feel a  quiver of danger from him but cannot yet see why.

'I say, the entire truth has not yet been revealed to us – not by the scriptures or by any other man-written authority. And I say, anyone who disagrees with me is a fool!'

There is audible rustle from the audience, including a man in black standing in the tier below me.

'True heretics are the men content to sit beneath a tree and say, "Do not try to enlarge man's knowledge" while they debate the error-ridden edicts of antiquity. Like parrots, squawk, squawk...'

'I will not stay to be insulted any further!' cries the man in black. 'Misled by your rumoured reputation, I came here to observe morbid anatomy, not to clap the antics of a heretical, foreign, Italian clown. Pray, excuse me.' He clambers over feet and sleeping dogs and climbs the steps to the exit. After a brief pause, two of my young men from the street argument follow him.

The doctor grins with apparent satisfaction. 'Two fewer than last time.' He lays one hand on the coffin. 'God does not keep the truth clutched to his chest as a closely guarded secret. All parts of all living things are as accessible to our eyes as a watch – every living thing on earth, in the sea and in the sky – mice, cats, dogs, eagles, weasels, elephants, starfish. Men. Women. Infants, even, when we can get them…if we look for ourselves.'

He nods. The two servants set aside the coffin lid and heave Henry's body onto the large table. Naked except for a small linen clout covering his genitals, Henry flops and wobbles like a drunk being put to bed.

'A multitude of wonders wait to be discovered by us.' The doctor contemplates Henry. We are all mesmerised by the corpse. 'But we must, surely, even so, arrive at the day when we will have examined every part of every creature, as we are about to examine this man. Then, and only then – by reason, not blind faith –  man will know all that God Himself – the Divine Clockmaker – knows about His perfect universe. By reason and by observation.' He holds black-clad arms wide to welcome us all into enlightenment.

Two more men in black leave.

'The only heresy is ignorance,' the doctor calls after them. He gazes at Henry and recovers his good humour. 'We are doubly fortunate today. Henry was hanged only this morning. And you have cooler weather here than in Italy where we must rush before the corpse can spoil – if we can get one at all.' He beams at the assembled crowd. 'In any case, I prefer to carry out my observations in a country where only some call me "heretic".'

The doctor now takes Henry's limp wrist. 'You will see that the muscles and bones are merely the ropes and levers. Operating thus...and thus.' He bends and straightens Henry's arm three times.

He turns to pick up a knife. He places his left hand on Henry's belly. 'Before your eyes, I will take apart the watch.'

# 7

The blade draws a neat red line down Henry's belly. 'First I divide the peritoneum in a straight line from the pectoral bone to the public bone.'

The edges of Henry's skin leap apart. The doctor's assistant wipes the red ooze with a sponge.

'Then, I cut transversely left to right, just above the tips of the hip bones. Now I liberate the *umbellicus*... thus...' The doctor is transformed. His face is now intent, his voice animated by contained excitement. He parts Henry's skin like a shirt.

I am transfixed.

'This milky membrane  beneath the skin is the *omentum,* which covers the eight abdominal muscles...'

I can't follow the Latin but catch the man's excitement as he prods, probes and snips.

A man in green silk in the second tier faints and has to be carried out. The doctor appears not to notice. His blade flashes as he points out with fervour the rich reds, blues, yellows and startling whites, as if they are a painting not the emerging wonders of the viscera.

Then the shift begins like the first stones in an avalanche. I stare at the gut, fallen apart with a final snip of the doctor's scissors. Like a string of sausages. Henry becomes meat on a butcher's table. The perfect machine is a wreckage, a tangle of membranes, tissues and bones. Where is the divine spark that animates it? Where is the place for the whispers and breathing of dark creatures in the underbrush.

I cling to the rail in front of me and try to steady my breathing, ambushed by a memory which has stayed hidden for years. The bill.

Grandmother had put me to bed in Amsterdam, not with lullabies but with tales choked by rage and tears. 'Your grandfather was burnt at the stake, by his own English people. For no greater crime than selling old-style Catholic books!' Her eyes had blazed. 'So that His Majesty, King Henry VIII, could disown his rightful queen, the blessed Katherine of Aragon, and marry that whore-witch, Nan Boleyn!'

She had shown me a bill when I was about six years old. 'Presented to me when I was only moments made a widow. And I had to pay! Here's for the wood that burned him...' She had pointed a trembling finger. '...and here's the fee for the man who lit it.. and there's the cost of the cart to carry away his ashes and the charred bits of bone. I prayed for him to breathe in the smoke and end his agony...I prayed for him to die!'

I cling to the rail and try to blot out an image. Before he was tied to the stake, she had said, my grandfather was dressed in a pitch-covered gown. I feel the flames. I am my grandfather burning at the stake. A dancing shadow, smoke searing my lungs, my hair flaring like dried grass.

My purpose here in England becomes suddenly clear. I am the only reason left alive for the lives of an entire family. My father and mother died of marsh fever. My grandmother is dead. I must live or it is the end of the Seabrights. I must give them purpose for having been on earth.

Here on the top wooden tier, I am possessed by a calm resolution. The name of my family's estate drums in my head: Seabright Hall. In Lincolnshire. I see the Seabright Crucifix, described by my grandmother, as if I held it. I will honour my vow to my grandmother and reclaim Seabright Hall, in all our names. But in order to do that, I must tear out my wolf. And prove it.

'...Observe how the venous structure, like internal rivers...Shining claret-hued kidneys...' The doctor splits them like exotic fruits.

Is this the right man to help me? I might have made an audible noise. The doctor's eyes find me briefly.

'And at last the liver.' He frees the wine-coloured organ and holds it aloft for everyone to see. 'Is this a five-lobed liver as your "Ancient Authority" would have it after dissecting a dog in place of man?' he demands. 'Or is it two lobes? Two lobes, not five! Look for yourself! Two. Not five! Man, not dog!'

He looks straight at me.

He thrusts the liver at a man in the lowest tier. 'Look! Is this heresy or truth?' I swear that he catches my eye. 'There is no darkness which the light of direct observation cannot reach!'

Physicians and scholars crowd round. People climb down from the tiers to see more closely. Henry's dark red liver is passed from hand to hand.

'Two. Indeed, only two...not like a dog at all!'

'I confess, I doubted.'

'...a triumph of reason.'

The doctor's eyes find mine again as if the message is for me alone. I balance between relief that he somehow knows the truth about me and blind fear. I can't decide whether or not to put myself into his hands.

Then I hear the dogs.

Careless of other people and pets, I fight my way to the doors at the top of the tiers. I think I hear the doctor shout, 'Wait!' but I can't wait to be taken again.

I throw myself down the stairs, run through the courtyard and out through the gate into the cobbled lane where Kat and I stood in the crowd before the demonstration.

Dogs pour into the far end of the lane, noses to the ground. At a distance still. No men visible yet. But no way to warn Kat! I sprint away from the dogs, but I know it's no use running if they have my scent. I stumble, curse the uneven cobbles, arrive at a riverbank.

Go left or right? Or straight ahead into the water?

The river embraces Cambridge here like an arm thrown around its shoulders. I take in details swiftly. Across the river are water meadows. The dogs will soon pick up my scent wherever I cross. On the near bank, people of all ages and sorts sit in the watery afternoon sun eating, reflecting, talking, debating. A few are in distant boats to my right. Ahead of me, a young woman soaks her feet, with petticoats drawn immodestly up to her calves. To my left the river is open, without cover. None of them notices me as they live their wonderful, ordinary lives. But I know that will all change when the dogs break out of the lane. Heads will lift, eyes will look at me...I don't know which way to run.

A cacophony of bells starts to ring, some near, some distant. A distant watchman calls in one of the colleges. The young woman begins to dry her feet. A boat turns in the distance and heads back this way. A group of youths stands and begins to put back on their folded black gowns. Their heads turn to me as I slide into the water to the left. The open river.

Unlike most English, I can swim. My grandmother made me learn because of the constant danger of falling into the Amsterdam canals. I dive now towards the only visible cover, an overhanging tree growing on the far bank. I swim underwater, surface among its branches, lungs bursting, spitting out leaves and dead insects. I yank at wet ties and struggle out of my sodden wool doublet, hook it over a branch, then, treading water, I remove the breeches. I snatch a look at the bank behind me. A man points at the water, then at where I'm hiding. Another waves to the nearest boat. Three dogs sniff at the ground on the other side of the water fifty feet away.

I can't stay here, but neither riverbank offers cover beyond my tree. The hailed boatman heads in my direction. Then I see a side channel upstream to my left, back across the river on the college side.

I inhale and dive again, deep, into a lingering winter chill, swimming towards the side channel.

Must breathe. Surface. Gasp at air and dive again. The light is fading but not fast enough. My dark head is visible against the water.

Dive again. One, two, three, four strokes. Gliding. Five, six...

*Where is that channel?*

I kick. I grope under the water at the mud of the left bank.

Suddenly, my left hand hits nothing. A gap.

Praying that it's the side channel, I turn, still underwater. Mud now below me as well as to either side. I

105

can't hold my breath any longer. I tilt my nose and mouth above the surface and blink water out of my eyes.

I have entered the side channel, a drainage ditch from one of the Colleges, from the jakes by the smell of it. The banks will hide me if I stay low enough. I don't know where the boat is. The dogs are very close on the near side.

I claw my way up the little stream. The banks become lower. I slither on my belly over slimy stones through the stench of the trickling current towards the possible safety of darkness and the maze of channels that I imagine running beneath the college. Where the dogs can't follow me through the water and stink. Then I see a half-moon grille of interlocking iron bars blocking the way. The ditch ahead of me passes through a barred hole in a wall. Water and filth flow through the grille out of the dark opening. Nothing larger that a rat or snake can get in.

I see the dogs approaching, noses to the ground. The bow of the boat is level with the channel entrance. Then the lead dog lifts its head from the ground and sees me.

I give up trying to hide. Dripping water, I climb out of the ditch. I'm on a narrow track. To my left, the track is blocked by a heavy, solid wooden gate into the college, twice as tall as I am. To my right, two armed men block the way. Across the narrow track is a wall.

Men run behind the dogs towards me. They see me now. I jump to try to pull myself over the wall on the far side of the narrow track. A musket fires; I miss my grip. Fall back. Turn to face the dogs.

Their nails clatter on the brick of the paved track. They now surround me. Their reek of triumph lifts the hairs on my neck. Ecstatic whoops echo off the wall behind me. I imagine their sharp yellow teeth stripping the muscle from my bones, dark red shining spots of blood splattering the wall as they yank at their prey.

A huge dog steps from the pack and stops three feet away. It has the rusty coat and lion face of an English mastiff. I stare down into its eyes, trying to hold it off with my will. The bloodshot eyes netted in sagging flesh hold a suppressed rage that it can never bite hard enough to relieve.

I set my back against the wall. My hand gropes for a weapon, closes on some wood. I glance at the wood – a length of it. I remember playing with dogs on the Amsterdam canal side as a boy, turning aside to placate an older, stronger dog. It is no use laying my head playfully on the ground. I understood dogs, even then. I am now the prey, and prey does not negotiate. If I were the demon-wolf, it would be a better match.

'Down, sir!' I bellow with all the human authority I can muster.

The mastiff rumbles at me in its throat. It lifts its lips from its black gums and bares white incisors as large as a boar's tusks. Hairs bristle at the base of its tail. Another growl rumbles from it throat, as deep as cartwheels on stone.

Two dogs step out of the pack to back it. The rest of them bay: *Howp! Howp!*

The mastiff advances n me with a swagger of shoulder. I gauge the power of those shoulders, the neck, the block-like jaw that was made to break an enemy's neck or strip the muscle from a bull's flank. How could man imagine that such a creature is subject to his will?

I clutch the length of wood. Get behind it, try to smash its skull...stun it...slow it...

Maybe lose a hand or knee. Or find myself lying on the bricks trying to suck air through a torn throat.

*Howp! Howp!* The pack bays in ravenous glee.

I glance towards the men who are just catching up with the dogs. More guns. More swords.

In that second of inattention, rusty fur and snapping teeth hit me. My piece of wood clatters to the ground.

'A sixpence on Brutus!' a man shouts.

'I wager a farthing on the other!'

The mastiff swings me like a rat. I hit the wall, scrabble for footing. Then it slams me back against its shoulder. Shirt sleeve and skin tear.

*Stay close. Stay out of its teeth. Get onto its back, behind the teeth. If I turn wolf, let it be now!*

The dog opens its jaws to take a new grip on me.

I fling myself onto its back, hug the thick neck with both arms, hold on, try to choke it, my face crushed against the bristling fur. Loose hairs and the blaring smell of its rage fill my nose.

The mastiff writhes. I begin to slide off its shoulders, around the tree trunk neck. Crushed against the side of my eye, I see foothills of black lip and gum, and bloody razor peaks of teeth. Bristles stab my mouth and nose. I open my mouth for air.

*Fight like the wolf!*

I catch hold with my teeth. Tighten my jaws.

Suddenly, I hit the ground. Hot blood burns my mouth and chin. I gag.

'Shoot!' shouts someone.

'Don't shoot! Take it alive for questioning!'

I lie, lungs heaving. Beside me, the mastiff quivers. Its hindquarters twitch while its life sprays out over the brick.

I cough and spit bristles from my mouth. I sit and wipe my chin and look at my hands - human hands, not claws. I stare blankly at my torn bloody sleeve which I've not yet begun to feel. At the dying dog.

I did that.

Or my wolf did it.

A circle of pointing muskets, swords and pikes forces me to my feet. I scrub at my chin with the sleeve of my good arm. I asked my wolf to come. I am not certain which of us killed the dog.

# 8

A sharp metal point pushes me forward, past piles of stacked stone and lead pipes in neat heaps.

I count my escort. Seven to one. Outnumbered.

Metal grates on metal. The gatehouse of a demolished castle now serves as a prison. A thick gate creaks open then slams heavily behind me. The noise from the street is suddenly muted.

My captors force me across a small inner yard. They acquire a torch. Down dark, cold stone stairs. Keys grate in locks. Last chance to try to escape.

How will Kat find me?

A sword point forces me through a low door. Chains rattle again. Several men chain me once more, on my back in a taut X so that I can't move. Wounds stretched. Wet clothes on a damp, cold stone floor.

The torch leaves with the men.

'No!' I shout.

The door closes behind them.

Total darkness.

Eyes closed, eyes open. No difference.

Nothing.

Darkness and silence. A smell of damp stone and the acrid dustiness of rats and mice. I strain to see the shapes that always emerge from the night: trees, houses, men, shadows on stones. Nothing. No lighter blackness of a window. No window slit for a demon to slide through. They are taking no chances this time. I am blind.

Kat will never find me now.

Invisible rats or mice scurry on the stone floor. Then they are silent, slipped out of the cell through a tiny hole.

If only my demon wolf had their skill.

Help me now! I beg it.

Demon wolf won't come.

My flesh chills in wet clothes on the damp stone floor of a cell never reached by sunlight. I start to shiver violently. My heart races. I've seen the last light I will ever see. They will leave me buried there, to die in the dark.

Dark. Can't bear it.

Must.

I try to escape into other thoughts...

Kat filching food. Eating a hot mutton pie, greasy and succulent, smelling of cinnamon and nutmeg...

What has happened to Kat? Have they arrested her too? Is she near me in a neighbouring cell?

My fault. What if Grillet claims her back? Accuses her of firing the hay barn to help me escape? Of being a witch? He will vent all his fear and anger on her, because I am out of his reach.

Please, let her have run!

Dark. So dark.

Time? No way to tell.

How long have I been here?

What do they mean to do to me?

The claws of invisible rats or mice scurry again on the stone floor. Then silence.

Darkness is as thick as water.

I must not go mad!

How would I know?

I turn my head to the sound of a key in the lock. A line of light widens as the door opens. My eyes hurt in the sudden light.

I look away from the jumping ball of flame. But I see...see! Stone walls...the shapes of three men... Delicious sight!

'Still looks chained fast.' The hushed voice of the guard with the torch.

The third man, his face hidden by wide-brimmed hat, smells of lavender and civet. He stands looking down at me. Orders the guard to hold the torch close to my face. I squeeze my eyes shut.

'It's him.' It might be the doctor's voice. His dark shape fingers my wrist. 'I'll have him.'

The two guards unlock my chains.

I sit up stiffly.

The guards jerk me to my feet and re-chain me, wrists together in front of me like the farmers but upper arms chained tight to sides. Enough slack between my feet to allow short steps. With a guard gripping each arm, I hobble, clanking, up the stone steps. The man with the hat climbs behind us, now holding the torch.

I remember the fresh corpse at the doctor's demonstration. Execution, I think. A secret hanging. Whatever is happening, it cannot be good. But it's almost worth it to be out of the dark.

We emerge in the small inner court of the guard house. I see the sky. It is night. Silent and deep. Not yet even false dawn.

The outer gate stands open. An unlit carriage takes up most of the space in the little courtyard, already turned to face the open gate and road. A pair of horses shift restlessly in the harness. Everyone hurries. Quiet voices. A single lantern lights the guard house.

The man in the black cloak and wide-brimmed hat - who might or might not be the doctor – hands a heavy leather purse to one of guards. The other guard watches the exchange carefully. Hands count coins in the lantern light. I see the bright yellow glint of gold.

The man in the hat looks into the road outside the open gate. 'Make haste, will you! I assure you, it's all there!'

A shadow moves. A familiar sweet smell. 'Rafe!' The whisper comes from the thick darkness near the inner wall.

With a glance at the distracted guards, I shuffle an eager step towards the whisper. 'You're free! How did you find me?'

'Listened for the dogs and followed.' The shadow moves closer. 'What's happening? Have they hurt you?'

'What are you doing here?' I can't lift my chained arms to touch her.

'Where are you going?'

'Don't know.'

'We need them chains back!' says one of the guards. 'He's supposed to have taken another shape, remember? And slipped out of them and escaped. So we have to leave them in the cell.'

'Take them then.'

Kat's shadow sinks back into the darkness. 'Wait…!' I whisper, but she is gone.

The two guards replace my chains with ropes around my wrists and ankles. Then they heave me headfirst into carriage.

'Don't damage him!' the man in the hat says sharply from behind them.

A pale hand grips the bottom edge of the dark window on the far side of the carriage.

I struggle to the door on that side. Kat's blonde head reaches to just below the window. I fumble at the door handle with bound hands.

The carriage rocks. The man gets in on the other side.

'Wait!' I say to him urgently.

We lurch forwards and begin to move. The narrow gateway arch echoes back the screech of wheels and thunder of horses' hoofs. The carriage grates against the arch wall. Then we are in the open air.

I lean precariously from the window. Kat has escaped unhurt through the arch. Her shape runs behind us, faster and faster to try to keep up with the increasing pace of the horses.

I throw all my weight on the handle, push the door half-open.

'Get in!' I yell. I lean out of the swinging door. She reaches for my bound hands, misses them, falls against a house wall, gasping for breath.

Hands haul me back inside the carriage. The man leans across me and slams the door.

'Stop!' I shout. 'We must take her with us!'

'I'll send for her later. At the moment, I'm trying to save your life.'

I am pushed down onto the carriage seat. I try to get to the door again. We wrestle. He is stronger than he looks and I am weakened by my injuries. At last, I sink back onto the seat. 'We must go back for her!'

There is a beat of silence filled only with our heavy breathing.

'Give me your hands.'

In the faint, intermittent light of the lanterns hanging outside passing houses, I see the gleam of a small blade.

After a moment, I hold out my hands.

Fingers probe delicately, find the rope. I feel pressure. Then my hands are free.

'Now your feet. Sit back and lift them up for me.'

Again, the blade winks in the passing light.

'Aren't you afraid to set me free?'

'I don't believe in so-called "magical" transformations.' The shape of the man puts away the knife. 'Get down on the floor under that blanket. The night watch is due on his round, any moment. You'll be seen.'

'We must go back for her!'

'I said I would send for her later.'

I put my head out of the window. The carriage rolls through a deserted street lit only by the lanterns hanging above closed doors. No one is abroad. Shadows move deep in an alley, but the carriage rolls on before I can see more. I hear the splash of a chamber pot emptied from an upper window.

No Kat.

'I said, lie on the floor and pull that blanket over you. I didn't pay all that money to have you retaken.' The man pushes me down onto the carriage floor. 'We must get you away from here with no one the wiser.'

'How will you send for her? Where are we going? I must tell her where we're going!'

'I said I'll send for her. Don't you want to live?' A passing lantern flashes on his face. It is the doctor.

'But how will you know where…?'

'Stay down on the floor! Talk later.'

He hides me with a blanket. I can't see anything beyond it. The grating of cobbles beneath the wheels turns to a smoother rattle, like on the stone of an old Roman road. Time blurs: werewolf, Alice Brinkley, Kat feeding me, the priest and his failed exorcism, flight with Kat, the burning hay barn, the placard, the doctor and his demonstration of the executed Henry's liver, the mastiff, killing it…too much.

He told me he will send for her…

Exhaustion hits me. In spite of myself, I sleep.

# 9

The wool blanket is brown in the early light. The doctor bundles it into a heap in a corner of the carriage.

It's dawn. I sit up blearily. Every muscle aches.

'It's safe to show yourself now. We're well away from Cambridge.'

I climb from the floor of the carriage onto the rear-facing wooden seat. I glance out of the carriage window. We travel north.

Teeth flash white in the growing light. 'Greetings, Master Seabright. Good day.'

I stare in confusion at the plump, eager face of a wrinkled cherub under a thick mop of dark grey hair, sharing a carriage with me. Pillowed cheeks catch the early light, puffed out in a grin. I inhale civet and lavender from his clothes as he leans towards me.

Nothing that has happened to me in the last four days feels real. I am an Amsterdam street rat. I will wake up any minute and wonder where my dreams of turning wolf have come from. But my throat still hurts from breathing in smoke. And the stink of my shirt is real enough.

'What's happening? I stretch carefully. The pain in my arm is real. And my back.

This doctor seems real, too. At least, he sits opposite me in a dark green-painted carriage that jolts convincingly over ruts in the road. I have not yet been executed to be used for one of his demonstrations of anatomy.

'Great projects!' The doctor spreads his arms, beaming, exposing his belt where he would have been carrying a sword. He seems unaware of my water-stiffened, mud-caked, stinking shirt and drawers. 'With your help. Together, we will topple ignorance from its present seat of power and drive it back into the wilderness where it belongs.'

He still wears the black of a scholar under his black travelling cloak. His white collar is askew. The growing light confirms his face. 'I will change the accepted Truth.' The man across the carriage beams at me again.

I feel I must get away.

'Although you know me, of course, as Dottore Giovanni Paduensis, I'm better known by my students here in England as plain "Dr John."' A modest pause. 'You too may call me that. As I said at my demonstration, I'm a New Philosopher, observing for myself. I've come to

England to pursue my observations. In Italy, the Catholic Church still manacles all seekers after knowledge...damns my work as "heretical".' He snorts in derision.

A wheel drops into a deep rut. The carriage lurches. I grab the edge of the seat to keep from being jolted back onto the floor.

The doctor nods. 'These country tracks could shake all sense loose from your skull.'

The ordinariness of his remark somehow reassures me.

'Did you pay to free me?' I am certain that I saw money change hands at the gaol.

The doctor waves the question away. 'It is the convention to do so in this country...as it is in mine.'

I am unchained. I can leap from the carriage. The doctor does not carry a sword to stop me. After another glance at the rising sun, I don't think we're going back to Grillet's estate. I touch my bitten forearm, now tender and swollen, and look at my shredded, bloody sleeve. I do not imagine the mastiff.

I shake my head to clear it and scrub at my chin with both hands. Kat pressed against me under the horse blanket...the warmth and scent of her... are surely real.

The sharp, sweet smell of the burning hay barn, and the orange flames that throbbed against the night sky…my escape from Grillet's farm had been real enough though my memory of it is hazy. All seems well enough for the moment, but I am uneasy.

How did the man across the carriage know to meet my eye during his demonstration? How did he find me again so quickly? I came to Cambridge to find a scholar. A scholar seems by a miracle to have found me – Doctor John of Padua who had observed the difference between the livers of dog and man. Whoever he may be, he enjoys the sound of his own voice far too much.

The doctor seems to read at least some of my thoughts. 'I had heard of you. And you attended my demonstration of anatomy yesterday…'

Those eyes had indeed found me in the crowd of onlookers. I did not imagine that either.

'You witnessed the size of my following. I should not be seeing the present doubt in your eye.' The doctor points at me in triumph. 'There! I was right! You are wondering whether I am a mad clown.' He leans forward and looks deep into my eyes. 'I assure you that I am neither mad nor clown. I mean to be Praelector of

Anatomy at the university in Padua. I know who you are, Master Seabright. I know what you did to the dog and what you are said to be. Together, we will learn the truth.'

The truth. I had come to Cambridge in search of it. I must know the truth. Return to my true self. The demon wolf tempts me with the power to defeat the mastiff; it tempts me with the power to hear and smell more than I did before, but I must be rid of it. It is also dangerous. 'Can you remove my wolf?'

The doctor's eyes narrow slightly. There is a heartbeat of silence. 'So long as it is not the delusion of a madman, I will find it,' he says. 'And if I can find it, I can remove it. Fear not. All will now be well. You are in the hands of a reasonable man.' He smiles again.

I wish he would not smile so much.

I look down in the early light at the raw red chafing of my wrists. I remember the absolute blackness of the prison cell where I thought I had been left to rot. I breathe in the damp, green-smelling spring air that drifts sweetly past my face into the growing light inside the carriage. Against all expectation, I am free. I might soon be freed from my wolf. By Reason. Not by superstition or death but by science and Reason. I can be myself again. My life can resume. I can seek Kat and live with her without danger. Excitement flickers inside me.

'All will be well,' he said. I want to believe him.

The carriage turns right. The track grows even rougher.

I gaze out of the carriage window and blink hard. The sky flushes pink. The sun rises ahead of us over the flat, wet fields. I see sharp blue-black shadows and vivid greens: an ordinary, lovely world I thought I had lost forever. I may be allowed to re-join it, with this doctor's help, all being well.

# 10

Just after the sun peaks at midday, the doctor gets down from the carriage to unlock a pair of heavy iron gates between high brick walls. He gets back into the carriage and smiles reassuringly. We turn through the gates down an avenue of elms.

'We have left Cambridge far behind,' the doctor says. 'I need solitude to think and study, and you will be safe from the ignorant mob.' He smiles again. 'The rest of today and tonight, you must eat and heal. Get a grasp on all that has happened to you. We will wait until tomorrow to begin our search for our answers.'

We roll into a cobbled forecourt at the end of the avenue between two inner gate posts topped with stone unicorns. No gatekeeper welcomes us.

He climbs down from the carriage a second time and waves for me to follow. 'Welcome, my fellow soldier in the army of Reason!'

The carriage and driver roll back up the avenue.

The doctor follows my eyes as they follow the carriage. 'Hired. I will lock the gates behind him later.'

We seem to be alone on an isolated estate deep in the country. No gatekeeper. No stable grooms required by the hired carriage. I am uneasy again.

The house is of brick with two wings receding at right-angles to the front. A protruding brick porch is raised by six steps above the courtyard. In the place of a porter, the female assistant from the demonstration opens the door.

'My new assistant, Jacobina.'

She takes the doctor's travelling cape and passes it to an elderly maidservant, the first servant that I've seen. After greeting us, Jacobina lowers her eyes but slants a quick look at me. I study her covertly. I inhale but can't read her smell.

She is as tall as she looked in the anatomy theatre, equal to the doctor's height. Tendrils of hair the colour of winter sunlight escape from under a plain, lace-free linen cap. Seen more closely, her clothes, though without ornament, are made of linen and fine wool.

She spreads her hands in welcome. The single maidservant retreats with the doctor's travelling cape. I follow the doctor through a wood-panelled entrance hall into the great hall of the house.

I stop dead and stare at the vast chamber, which could once have seated an entire house family at meals. I smell ghosts of banquets held here, the important guests received at long tables ranged down the middle of the room.

Now tables of all sizes clutter the floor. Book-filled shelves line the walls in place of hangings, interrupted by occasional unframed maps and diagrams attached by a corner or three while the other corners flap. Stacked papers slide askew on every surface. Dirty steel knife blades mingle with jars of pickled specimens floating in liquid. Two live snakes twist sinuously together in a large glass jar next to a half-burnt candle anchored to the table by a puddle of wax. Though the late spring day outside is filled with bright green and sunlight, the high-ceilinged hall is damp and shadowed in spite of a small fire burning in a fireplace large enough to stable a horse.

I raise my eyes. A withered crocodile hangs from the wheel-like, rusted iron candleholder above our heads.

The doctor waves his arm happily. 'Here, I work to bring order from the chaos of Nature. Here, we will work together to throw light on your wolf and remove it.' He parts the neck of my shirt and touches my skin. 'For example, your breastbone is wide, while a wolf's is scarcely a palm's breadth across. I can already see, on the other hand, that your legs are long in proportion to your torso and your feet large – body traits of a wolf...'

Perhaps all scholars work in such a chaos of books and papers. I don't know any others.

'For shame, sir, your guest hasn't even had refreshment yet,' his assistant, Jacobina, interrupts. She wipes a poker from the fire on a square of leather.

'Master Seabright is not a guest; he is a colleague!' retorts the doctor. 'I have rescued him from execution by Superstition and Unreason. I will restore purpose to him by enlarging human knowledge.'

She puts the hissing poker into a mug of ale then hands me the warmed ale. The heat eases my scorched throat. I gulp it down.

'Slowly.' The doctor sounds amused. 'Your body needs time to grow re-accustomed to food and drink.'

I cup the warm curve of the pewter mug in my palm. Then I press it against my face and remember Kat's hand, also warm, also comforting, pressed against my cheek. Will she be able to track the carriage to this isolated house? The doctor has promised to send for her, but how will he know where to find her? Will she want to come?

The world feels increasingly dream-like. Thoughts of Kat grow blurry. My nightmare flight from death seems to be over for the moment. I drain the last of the warmed ale.

'Now, before we dine like civilised men, you must bathe… you do have a certain doggish smell about you.' The doctor smiles to soften any possible offence. 'Go with Jacobina.' He begins to clear space among the papers and mysterious instruments on one end of a long table.

'Like civilised men…' The words echo in my head as I hand back the pewter mug. '…civilised…' Then I consider 'doggish smell'. Is that a civil way of saying, 'wolfish'? I sniff surreptitiously at my armpits, smell the stink of the drainage ditch. I wonder again how far my demon wolf is entwined into my flesh.

Jacobina leads me up a creaking dog-legged wooden staircase in the entrance hall. She stops to open a door and steps back. 'This will be your sleeping chamber while you are here.' She looks as if she wants to say more, then waves me through into a wood-panelled room, simple but bright, holding only a four-poster bed, a clothes press, and an upright iron bathtub in front of a small fire burning in the fireplace. She closes the door. I hear her footsteps creak back down the stairs,

The elderly female servant has filled the upright, metal tub. I sniff my armpits again. The doctor is right. I stink like an animal. 'With your permission,' I say to the maidservant, who turns away to the fireplace. I strip off my torn, muddy shirt and drawers, too weary for modesty, and climb into the tub.

Every hair on my body prickles with mixed pleasure and pain as I lower myself slowly in the hot water up to my chest. I sit stewing delightfully, knees folded, feeling the fire on my face, while the woman – still the only servant I have seen so far – pours jugs of heated water over my head and shoulders. Each sluicing sends cascades of thrills running through my chest and belly. The hot water burns the whip lashes on my back and the bite on my arm, but my aching muscles loosen. I sigh. If it was Kat pouring the jugs of hot water over me, I would want nothing more.

I drift and dream. She might even climb into the tub with me. Then I would pour water over her and make the hairs on her arms stand up in wonder at the sheer bliss of it all.

Suddenly, I am erect. I cover myself with my hands and pray that the old maidservant has not noticed. Grandmother would have beaten me for my wicked thoughts, but she is dead and my world is changed.

The maidservant has turned back to the fire where more water warms and seems to have seen nothing.

'That's enough,' I tell her.

She shrugs and begins to turn back the bedcovers.

I duck my face into water that is wonderfully free of leaves and dead insects. Then I sink beneath the surface, feeling my hair float up and my bones lighten. Though aching for Kat and in spite of my uneasiness, I feel temporarily safe for the first time since I arrived in England.

'By your mercy.' The old woman leaves.

I soak until the water begins to cool. Then I scrub my face and arms with a linen towel that smells like sunlight.

As I dry my head on another towel, I eye the four-poster bed. I touch the clean sheets and feather quilt and stroke the soft goose down pillows. Must wait until after eating, but then...

I am suddenly too weary to think further of Kat.

A soft, clean, dry shirt and trousers lie folded on the bed; a pair of woollen stockings and soft leather house slippers stand on the floor. I put trousers, stockings and slippers. They fit neatly.

Before I can put on the shirt, Jacobina returns to bandage the dog's bite and smooth a dark, sweet-smelling ointment onto my back. Her fingers leave a trail of numbness and relief. She shows no sign of her former intention of speaking beyond the necessary instructions. She leaves again and I finish dressing.

When I return to the great hall, the doctor pushes aside a pile of papers. He waves me to a padded stool on one corner of the longest table while he takes the high-backed, carved oak chair-of-grace at the end. Jacobina sits on a stool opposite me. The same elderly servant who poured my bath now enters and re-enters, bringing us food. She places it in gaps left among the papers.

Surely a house this grand would have a slew of servants, not just the one, I think.

'I hope our food pleases you.' The doctor glows with delight at his new guest and colleague. 'Eat! Eat!'

I notice his eyes watching me curiously as I attack roast pigeon, chicken soup with ground almonds, saffron beans, stewed pears and baked apples. I try to eat slowly but gulp the food, as if it might be snatched away at any moment.

'Which dish do you prefer?' he asks.

'Do let him eat a few bites before you start your questions!' The assistant's tone is light.

The doctor ignores her and repeats his question.

'I like… all of it.' I swallow a piece of succulent chicken. I remember my manners. 'How can I ever thank you, sir?'

He waves a dismissing hand. 'I am grateful to *you*, Master Seabright, for joining me in scientific partnership.'

I lose myself in the wonders of a baked apple – soft but not liquid, cool on my tongue, flavoured with cinnamon and honey.

'Do you always fill your stomach as if against a long fast?' the doctor asks. 'How long can you go without eating?'

Jacobina knocks over her wine glass.

I use my napkin to dam the crimson flood that threatens to spill over the table edge onto the floor. I feel the weight of a gaze and look up to catch the doctor watching us both intently as Jacobina finishes mopping up the spill. Then the aging cherub's face smiles. 'No harm done in the end.'

We begin to eat again, in silence now. As my hunger eases, I gaze curiously around the room while I chew. I decide that those jars of pickled specimens are slightly sinister, holding unidentifiable bits that might once have been alive.

The doctor must have followed my eyes. 'I see that you share my sense of wonder at all that Nature holds for us New Philosophers to examine. Look there!' Gleefully, he points at the two live, slowly twining snakes. 'The Classical authorities insist – against the evidence of their own eyes – that those two creatures are the same, but I have proved by simple observation that they differ!'

My eyes linger on a blunt pickled shape floating in another jar. 'What is that?'

There is a tiny pause. 'The heart of a changeling,' he says lightly. 'A monster.'

I stare a moment longer. The thing in the jar looks very much as I imagine the heart of a child.

As I begin to eat again, a skin-tingling howl freezes me with my spoon tilted in a second portion of chicken and almond soup. It comes from close by within the doctor's estate, desperate and chilling. The long tendril of sound climbs step by step. The stretched eerie notes bore into my marrow and pin me through the heart.

The doctor turns to his assistant. 'Silence it!'

She does not move.

'It's an ordinary wolf,' he assures me. 'As ordinary as the fleas on its neck, nothing like your internal beast. Bought from a travelling menagerie...rescued, I should say. Born in captivity. Never learned to hunt...needs to be fed.' He brushes a few crumbs into a pile by his plate. 'You've never seen such a poor, flea-bitten creature until Jacobina nursed it back to health with her herbs and potions. It's far happier now.'

The wolf howls again. It sounds to me like a howl of utter misery.

As if set off by the wolf, a scream suddenly pierces the evening, followed by another and another with scarcely a pause to draw breath. They sound very human. A girl's voice.

He raises his brows. 'The whole menagerie is giving voice tonight. Perhaps you might administer a quieting draught before our neighbouring farmers work themselves into a frenzy of fear for their livestock.'

The screams continue. 'Who is that?' I demand, suddenly afraid.

'A creature little more than a monkey, an ape...less than an ape. Nothing to do with your case.' The doctor looks at his assistant, who has not moved from her place. 'Why do you wait? Make yourself useful.' He smiles. 'You know that I can't do without you.'

Jacobina lifts her head. A strange chilling look passes between them.

When she is gone, the doctor returns to cracking a walnut. A little later, the screams die. The wolf does not howl again.

'That's better.' He leans back in his chair, chewing the walnut meat. He beams at me. 'Jacobina is a gifted apothecary. I don't know what I will do without her when she leaves me, as one day she will.' He leans across the table to refill my wineglass. 'Tomorrow, we begin the search for your wolf.' He raised his glass in a toast.

I raise my own. I push the howling and screams from my mind. Exhaustion and wine weigh down my eyelids though the sun has not yet set. Even trying to be civil to my host is not keeping me awake.

He smiles. 'I can see your eyelids drooping. Go! Go!'

Barely excusing myself, I shuffle back up the dog-leg stairs.

Alone in my sleeping chamber, I give a groan of bliss and sink belly-down into the feather and down mattress. Softness cradles me. My head seems to float on a sea of down. I stretch my battered feet to the charcoal-filled warming pan at the bottom of the bed – a luxury this late in the year but welcome in the dank brick house. My first bed since arriving in England. And my first four-poster, ever. With curtains, goose-down pillows and a feather-filled silk quilt.

'All will be well,' the doctor says. My supposed rescuer. I want desperately to believe in him. He says he will find my wolf, if it exists – and I know it does - and remove it forever. I am confused. My body starts to shake.

I don't know what to do. Is it the demon wolf speaking? Do I run now? Do I stay? I must be rid of my demon, but it helped save my life in the fight with the mastiff, I think though I can't be certain. On the other hand, I will never be safe while it is in me, must never see Kat again. The doctor is a renowned scholar. I've seen the audiences he attracts. I am only an Amsterdam street rat. He has reassuring answers for all my questions so far.

With the doctor, I am embarking on a lucid, rational march from ignorance into knowledge. Refusing his examination of my wolf will throw me back into darkness and confusion. If I trust him, I will put myself in the hands of Reason.

I will think about it in the morning. I sigh, turn onto my side and fall instantly asleep.

The creak of the door hinges wakes me.

Foggy with sleep, I reach under the pillow for my knife. Then I remember. I no longer have one. The footpads stole it, along with my purse, lute and clothes.

Heart thumping I watch a shadow ease the door open. The door creaks closed again. I lie still, but my muscles coil for action. The shadow slips silently to the side of my bed. Faint light gleams on loose white-blonde hair, no longer restrained by a cap. As far as I can see, she holds only an unlit candle-lantern in the slim strong hands that mopped up the spilled wine and stroked the salve onto my back. She appears to be wearing only her shift under a shawl.

I sit up and pull the down-filled quilt farther over my lap. My coiled muscles relax a little bit but not entirely. 'What are you doing here?' I ask quietly. It feels like the hushed bottom of the night.

'Are you awake enough to listen?' Her shape looks over its shoulder at the door. 'You must run tonight...'

My body clenches again. I interrupt in a fierce whisper. 'No! Decided not to run. Outside this house, men want to kill me. Hunt me. I'm a treason against nature. The doctor claims he will put me right.'

'The doctor lies,' she retorts with equal ferocity. 'He's interested in you but not as you think. Did you note his questions at supper? He can't contain his curiosity till tomorrow. He's already comparing you to a wolf. "Yes, this boy has large hands and feet. He gorges himself just as wolves gorge until their stomachs are full, so that they can go for a long time without eating again."'

'He saved me from execution!' But I think of the freshly executed Henry. And the underlying smell of blood in the great hall that I had refused to think about until now.

There is a distant cough.

'He's coming,' she mouths. She presses deep into the curtains of my bed as the crack beneath the door grows lighter. Feet approach. They shuffle past. The crack beneath the door darkens again. The footsteps go down the creaking stairs. 'Jacobina?' the doctor's voice calls from the hall below.

She reappears from the shadows. 'He saved you because he intends worse,' she whispers near my ear. 'He will make you want to die.'

'I'm not a complete fool. I know that scientific curiosity lies under the doctor's kindness. He observes for himself, as he says.' I will not think about the smell of blood.

'Jacobina?' calls the doctor's voice more distantly. 'I've had a thought, want to test it with you.'

'The New Philosophers – which he claims to be – are right to observe for themselves, but he goes too far!' she says.

'I know his scientific curiosity goes as far as finding and ridding me of my monster wolf.' My resolve strengthens again. 'I will learn how in the morning. I can handle his curiosity.'

'Why you think he has a captive wolf waiting? You heard it howling at dinner...Lie down! He's coming back! And I'm not in my room...' This time, she disappears into the shadows beyond the clothes press. I lie back down.

The doctor remounts the stairs. He coughs outside my door. Presses down the handle. The door opens quietly. A shadowy head appears. Listens. 'Jacobina?' it whispers. 'Are you in here?' It listens again.

With effort, I breathe steadily then sigh as if in sleep.

The doctor listens a little longer then withdraws. The door closes. The light of the man's candle fades from the crack beneath my door. Then I hear faint coughs after he closes his own door.

Jacobina reappears. 'He will be writing now,' she breathes. 'The doctor is unaware of trifles like night and day when pursuing an idea.'

We wait in silence, but the doctor stays in his room. I want to bury my head in the covers. I don't want to hear what I already know she is going to say.

'He means to compare you with the wolf in every detail,' she whispers. 'He will cut and slice in order to learn where you are wolf and where you are not.'

I clench my hands on the coverlet.

'You are merely a specimen for him to examine. He won't stop until his exploration has killed you - as it has killed all his previous specimens.'

'How do you know what the doctor intends?'

'Because I make the numbing salves and potions he will use.' I hear her swallow. 'And because I'm one of his waiting specimens.'

I sit back up.

'Right now, he needs me...and knows I have nowhere else to go. Ever since I first came here and understood what he intends, I've tried to make myself too useful to kill. But I don't deceive myself that I will escape his attention.'

'I don't believe you!'

'He'll find another assistant to sweep away the bloody sawdust and remove the fragments that remain after he has satisfied his curiosity on me. Someone to make his salves and potions.' Her shadowy mouth twists. 'Meanwhile, he thinks me willing to give myself to slake his thirst for learning – most of all, he cannot believe that I am willing to go on living as I am.'

"As you are?"

There is a pause. '

You haven't guessed?' she asks.

I shake my head.

She listens at the passageway again then turns the key in the door. She lights her candle lantern from the banked coals of the fire and sets the lantern on the shelf at the foot of my bed inside the curtains. She touches her first button. 'Do you mind?'

I shake my head again but my heart thuds.

She begins to undress.

My face goes hot as she drops her shawl on the floor. My heart speeds up. I want her to stop and I don't want her to stop.

She unbuttons her linen chemise and hauls it over her head. She stands completely naked, holding out her arms to invite inspection. 'How can the doctor resist the chance to anatomise this?'

Above the waist, she is a lovely young woman, below the waist, a youth.

I stare.

'What do you see?'

I have never seen anything like this creature, never even imagined it possible. I am surprised by my lack of horror or revulsion. But what I see is not horrifying. It is strange and mysterious, like something from a dream.

The male parts look as soft and unused as a baby's foot. With smooth hairless skin, pink and cream, the creature standing by the foot of my bed might be one of the angels, whose gender had always been unclear.

'Am I a monster?' asks Jacobina.

'Strange, but beautiful. Not monstrous at all!' I hear the astonishment in my own voice.

'All parts work perfectly well.' Jacobina turns to show wide shoulders a slim waist and ambiguous hips. 'I'm two creatures in a single body, like you. But there's no room for doubt in my case. I'm a "treason against nature," just as you say you are. But I have accepted it. Can you not do the same? Accept what you are?'

'If I were as beautiful as you...'

The creature sits on my bed, skin dyed to a golden peach by the lantern light. 'Can you not think the same about yourself – as strange but beautiful? If you could find a way to survive, could you not accept living in ignorance, as I do, about why and how you are different?'

'But we're both still monsters. And in danger. You can't deny it.'

Jacobina smiles. 'But isn't it a consolation to know that you're not alone, a solitary horrid blot on Creation?

That there are more of us in this world, others who are different, not just in travellers' tales and books? That we have a fellowship, and, somehow, we survive.'

'I'm not like you,' I protest. 'The beast inside me – my wolf – has nothing beautiful about it. It's evil and dangerous!'

'There are many ways of seeing. You might change your opinion even if you can't change that of the world.'

'Never! I can't change what I know.'

'I once felt as you do.' The lower male half settles itself squarely cross-legged on the striped bedcover. The upper female part tucks a strand of pale hair behind its ear and leans towards me.

I stare from male to female parts, still with disbelief. Jacobina seems lodged so securely in the world that I feel, in my disbelief, as if I'm the one who isn't real.

'The doctor often walks about while he works at night...' The whisper is muffled by the curtains of the bed. 'I may not have long, so pay attention.

'Because of these...' The creature gestured at its genitals. '...I seemed male when I was born and was raised as a boy for the first eleven years of my life.' She... he...looks away into the shadows. 'But as soon as I became aware – aged about three – that there were only two decreed sexes, male or female, I knew that I carried a dreadful secret: I was a double creature, both male and female at the same time, just as you feel that you're both man and beast, like mud and water trampled together.

'I saw what happened to people who were even slightly different. Heard children with twisted backs or shrivelled limbs cursed as treason against God's perfect universe. Or called the devil's spawn...'

I think fleetingly of Kat.

'...I saw them locked away or killed at birth. I was terrified that someone would guess the awful truth. At any moment, someone might point at me. So I ran faster, chopped more wood, and lifted heavier weights than other boys. I imitated their swaggering and rough language. I tried to like their games. I did not dare make a close friend lest a hint of the truth slip out.

'Then, when I was twelve, I sprouted these.' She gestures at her chest. 'I tried to hide them, bound them, but in the end I was exposed to the world for what I am.'

There is a moment of silence.

'My father decided one night to smother me in my sleep.' Jacobina looks at me for the first time since beginning her story. 'You must understand his position. I was a danger to the family, the source of malevolent gossip. Sooner or later, someone would attack me. Attack the family. In his place, I would have done the same, chosen the merciful way…'

A cramp bites into my gut. I don't believe her calm acceptance of her father's murderous intent.

'My mother guessed what he intended, gave me a ring, a silk jacket, a little money and bread – and smuggled me away while he was milking the cows that evening. I never saw her again.

'I left our village, found work in London as a maidservant …twice. The first time, the master groped. The second time, another servant spied on my bath. I gave up pretending. Flung myself among the lowest creatures in the city to await the destruction I knew must come – and that I felt I must somehow deserve.

'To my surprise, I prospered. My monstrosity won me a following in the inns and taverns among men of jaded appetites. And they kept me safe from those who would have cleansed the world of imperfection. Even so, from time to time, I thought of throwing myself into the Thames.'

'I deserve destruction far more than you,' I say. 'I...my beast... may have killed a child.'

'Do you remember doing it?'

'No. But I remember killing a dog.'

'Was the dog attacking you?'

I nod.

I doubt if the child was trying to kill you.'

Suddenly I don't know just how monstrous I really am. 'The doctor promised to find the beast inside me.' I hear my uncertainty. 'And remove it.'

'While you and the wolf are both alive. The dead soon spoil. We stay fresh for longer whilst we still live. He will dissect you while you are still alive. That way, he can take his time.'

My bones turn to ice. I imagine watching my own death.

She points down into the darkness in the hall below. 'Did you see the jars? The things floating in them were once parts of living creatures. Each one of them was different in his or her special way. The doctor searched for the secret of that difference, to satisfy his insatiable curiosity by "observing" for himself – while they were still alive.'

'I won't believe you!'

'Then why are you so angry?' Jacobina slides off the bed and begins to pull her shift back over her head.

'If it's true, why have you not fled?'

Her head reappears. 'You can see for yourself. Even the doctor must sleep some time.' She picks up her shawl then listens at the door. After a long time, she nods. 'Come meet my reasons.

I throw on my clothes silently. I don't need her to warn me to be quiet as we feel our way down some back stairs.

# 11

We move silently across the cobbled yard at the back of the house to the barn on the far side. Jacobina eases open a small hinged door set into the large barn door. She listens once more to the darkened house, we slip through, she closes the little door again.

Moonlight through an open hatch in the barn roof silvers the outlines of eight cages, set about eight feet apart. I breathe in scents: male, female, young, older, feral, rotting meat, stale food, urine, animal faeces, and dusty hay. Under it all, I smell an unfamiliar, sweet, brownish chemical odour.

I see human shapes in three of the cages. Touched by the moonlight, two heads turn towards us.

'Who's he?' demands a deep, adult male voice.

'These are the doctor's specimens,' says Jacobina quietly. 'Waiting, like you, to be examined.'

The deep voice comes, disconcertingly, from a caged shape no taller than my waist. 'What's this fine fellow doing here?' The little man grips the front bars of his cage to take a closer look at me. Chains rattle. 'Come to gawp, sir? To show off your fine, long legs? If you care to stay, there's a cage waiting for you, over there.'

I move closer, trying to see him more clearly. He smells musty and rich with age.

'Rafe Seabright, meet John Butters,' says Jacobina. 'Rafe's said to be a werewolf and accused of murder. Newly arrived. Doesn't need caging. He still believes that the doctor has rescued him.'

'A werewolf? Will he eat us?' asks the small shape with the deep male voice.

'I think not.'

'I wish I could welcome you, Rafe Seabright.' The small man, Butters, laughs sourly. 'I, too, once believed the doctor had rescued me. Offered me a position as his steward. I was tired of the only thing most people think dwarves fit to do – acrobatics and tumbling. Getting too old. Came willingly – does that not defy belief?' He turns to Jacobina. 'Have you brought more devil's brew to keep us quiet? The two you dosed earlier still sleep. Is it my turn now?'

'Jacobina?' The male voice comes from a second cage.

'And this is Dob.'

I move to the second cage and nod tentatively. In the moonlight, I see that his mouth is a split muzzle like a sheep or goat. Apart from his mouth, Dob seems built like an ordinary youth of about my age but shorter and stockier. He smells of sweat and hay. Strong hands grip the bars of his cage. Large gentle eyes catch the moonlight as he studies me.

'I, too...I came to work for the doctor...as...' Dob pauses to seek words.

'Dob's former master made him sleep from infancy in a barn,' says Jacobina. 'Claimed that Dob was half-animal and deserved no better.'

Dob slaps himself lightly in mock punishment.

'He has a gift with animals. Raised by them and among them, he speaks their tongues.'

I look curiously at her. 'Did the doctor deceive you as well?'

She shakes her head. 'Implied threats in my case. "I know your secret" he told me. And he smiled that smile of his. "Come work with me; I need your skills. I won't betray you. You will be safe with me."'

Abruptly, Jacobina moves to a third cage. 'This one had no choice. About thirteen, I reckon. Her father gave up on locking her away and sold her kicking and screaming to the doctor. He swore that she was not the child born to him. His true child, he said, had been stolen from her cradle and replaced by an evil spirit. Everything she touched was cursed, he said. The doctor offered him a way out of facing the truth. The girl is to be his next changeling.' She checks the girl's mug of water.

I remember the child-like heart in the jar.

'The doctor intends to take her apart to determine how much of her anatomy is demon and how much, human.'

'Father'd have done better to smother her,' murmurs Butters.

I peer into the cage. As far as I can see, the girl lying asleep on the floor looks nothing like the horrid devil child the word 'changeling' conjures up. Pretty under her dirt and tangled hair. She wears a dress which, though torn and crumpled, glows with the sheen of silk.

'A fine carriage delivered her about a month ago,' says Jacobina. 'And that's a costly dress. The letter 'O' was embroidered on her handkerchief, so we call her "Lady Olivia". She can't or won't speak.'

'Why is her mouth moving?' I ask.

'Still counting,' replies Butters. 'She counts the bars of all our cages again and again. Every day since she arrived.'

Jacobina squats with a sharp waft of black dye and wool and reaches between the bars to put fingertips on the girl's pulse. 'She screams so fiercely and so often that I fear the doctor will lose patience and kill her just to keep her quiet.' She frowns through the bars. 'But I may kill her first with an overdose of opium.'

The girl stirs in drugged sleep and settles again. Her dark silk dress humps up around her. One bare white leg sticks out. I see a pearl ring glinting on one long white finger. Jacobina stands again but remains beside the cage.

I stare down at the sleeping 'Lady Olivia', the supposed changeling.

'No doubt, he hopes to prove with observation that a changeling is a demon exchanged for a human babe, or else that it is not. I had not yet arrived here as his assistant, but I believe he found his first dissection inconclusive. You saw the jar at supper, the one he called "changeling".'

Bile rises in my throat.

'We're the menagerie of human monsters he will "observe for himself".' She moves to a fourth cage. 'Over here is his one true animal. Poor thing. Its time has come, with yours. As you heard at his demonstration, the difference between man and dog is an obsession of his, and between them lies the werewolf – both man and canine. As you are supposed to be.'

In the cage, a wolf lies stretched on its side, looking enormously long. A real wolf, not my demon one. At our approach, it half-raises its head groggily and snarls. I see a glint of pale teeth as long as my thumb before it drops its head again.

'Our howler. Your animal self.' Jacobina stoops to study it thoughtfully. 'It wakes too soon this time. It's hard to know – not enough drug in its meat and the doctor is enraged by its howls. Too much and I kill it.'

'Mistress Jacobina is Our Lady of Sleep,' the deep voice of Butters breaks in. 'She knows how to dose us all into obedience. "Whose turn is it now?" I ask every time I see her. She keeps promising us escape but we all are still here, with our time running out! Can we trust the food she brings, can we trust *her*?' He shakes his chains. 'I could open these locks if only she would bring me a good set of picks. She could do it, I'm certain. She walks about freely enough.'

'The doctor checks the locks regularly to prevent any attempt to escape,' Jacobina says mildly.

'Do you not have keys to the cages?' I ask.

'Do you think we would all still be here if I did?' She sounds angry for the first time.

The wolf is now trying to stand.

'The doctor will begin to compare Rafe with the wolf in the morning.' Jacobina tells the others.

'No, no,' murmurs Dob.

'Hurrah! That means I will live at least one more day!' Butters's chains rattle as he grips the bars of his cage. 'Your case must interest him greatly. I must study how to appear even more tedious.'

'Rafe is free only because the doctor believes he's ignorant of what lies ahead for him. I'm trying to persuade him to run tonight while he still can.'

'If I slip away tonight, he will know you warned me. What will he do to you...and the rest of you?'

'One survivor is better than none,' says Butters. 'Though, to be honest, I'd rather come with you.'

'Wouldn't we all!' says Jacobina.

'Wha' of Livia?' Dob asks suddenly. 'She, too.'

Butters turns on Dob. 'We can't take her even if we do get free. Pursuers would need only follow her screams.'

'Take her!' Dob is stubborn.

They argue as if I have already made the decision to flee. I realise that their lives hang on my decision. I bolt outside into the cobbled yard. Jacobina follows me. 'Even so, I can't go on as I am!' I whisper desperately.

She seizes the sleeve of my good arm. 'You haven't heard my whole story yet. One day, a man hauled me off a customer's lap in an inn. "I am your guide through the flames and back to life," he said. My head thought he was mad – and I didn't like the sound of those flames – but my feet followed him out of the inn.' She glances towards the house and the doctor. The moon comes from behind a cloud, lighting her hair and face.

'He was an alchemist, a true one – not one of those frauds who seek only to make gold. He had knowledge of plants and minerals, taught me all I know about herbs and potions – knowledge that keeps me alive for now.'

I try to pull away, but her grip tightens on my sleeve. 'Listen to me! He taught me to see my double being, not

158

as a monster but as an earthly form of the unknowable. The soul of the world, he said, which is neither male nor female yet encompasses both.'

I try to pull away again. I shake my head.

'He was my master until he died and taught me a lesson that made me forget throwing myself into the Thames. "There is room in the truth," he said, "for the unknowable as well as for the mechanical observation of Reason."'

'Are you telling me to accept my beast?'

'I offer you another shape for the truth.' She holds tightly to my sleeve as I struggle wildly. 'Hush!' she says.

I stop struggling but remain poised to run.

'I beg you to accept that you may never understand the mystery of your nature. To accept. You may always question what is good and what is evil. Dob's mother was accused of mating with the devil in the form of a hare. And was hanged as soon as he was out of her belly. Was that good? Is he evil?'

I look back at the stable in an agony of confusion. 'The doctor can't kill those people in there. Or you!'

'So, we're no longer demons or monsters? You already begin to see with different eyes. You must look with the same clarity at yourself.'

My head has too much in it. I fear it will burst. 'I can't!'

'Please don't force me to take part in your dissection. Don't make me rub you with numbing salve so you won't feel the knife.'

'Who will guide me through the flames?'

'I will,' she says. 'If you will trust me.'

My heart swells against my ribs. If I have observed for myself, if I believe the evidence of my own eyes, nose and ears, I have only one choice... deal with my wolf later. 'Escape, all together.'

Jacobina lets out a deep breath of relief.

'What must I do?'

'We'll run tomorrow night. Stay alive tomorrow until nightfall. It's the chance we need. You and the wolf distract the doctor's attention while we unlock the cages and prepare our flight. Be so fascinating that that you make him forget the rest of us. You must make him forget to check the cages – Butters will finally get his pick-locks and the time to use them...'

'Jacobina!' The doctor's shout is distant but imperious.

She glances in alarm towards the house. 'He's looking for me in earnest. I'll go round to the front, tell him I went walking in the avenue. When you hear us, sneak back to your room by the back stairs we came down. We will escape after his final lock-check. He will at least retire to his room after supper...I'll figure it out.'

She turns to run but says over her shoulder, 'He'll do surface observation first – measurements, both you and the wolf, legs, ears...temperature...Use every device in your power to slow him until dusk when the light begins to fail and he can't any see clearly any longer. He relishes debate. Distract him with debate. Once he begins to cut, it will be too late.' She vanishes into the darkness towards the front of the house.

I wait until I hear his voice calling her more faintly in the cobbled yard where the carriage arrived only this afternoon. Then I return up the back stairs to my room. My responsibility for all of them keeps me awake for what remains of the night.

161

# 12

I force myself to smile at the doctor over breakfast bread and cheese. I fear that he can smell my fear.

'To our partnership!' The doctor raises his mug of watered ale.

I smile back at him and raise my own mug. I delay as long as I dare. I yawn, explaining our late start.

Jacobina holds a wriggling mouse by the tail and drops it into the snakes' jar. 'Buy time,' she said last night. Distract the doctor so that he forgets to make his daily rounds, testing the cage locks and making certain that his captives are dosed into quiet. I must be fascinating. Fill his thoughts so that he forgets all else. Buy the rest of them time.

She sits opposite me again, eyes down, and begins to eat calmly. How can she seem so calm?

I break my bread into twenty small pieces and chew each one until it turns liquid in my mouth while I try to think how to appear fascinating. I still have five pieces left when the doctor leaps to his feet impatiently, drains his mug and slams it on the table.

'We must begin!' He pushes aside his plate and sets an open book in its place. I glimpse a page with a title written across the top and the drawn outline of a man, front and back. 'We have much to do today.' He lays out an ivory measuring rod and a pair of pincers.

I yawn again to explain my tortoise-like speed. 'I hope you will explain as we progress. I want to understand everything we do.'

The doctor nods. 'I knew you were more than just a subject for examination. A true scholar longs for a student like you. You are a rare creature, Master Seabright – both explorer and the explored.'

I shove my hands under the table at the word 'explored'. 'Where do we begin?' I ask in a voice whose steadiness surprises me.

I have no idea how much the doctor will do before he starts to cut me.

'First, we record all your surface details. Jacobina will measure. I will record.'

Jacobina keeps her eyes fixed on the table.

But she needs to prepare for their escape, I think.

*Do not look at her...*

'I must warn you' he says, 'that in the interests of the New Philosophy, I will take liberties with your person. I must ask you first to remove your clothes.'

Thinking fast, I say, 'I prefer not to undress before a woman. Can't I help you in Jacobina's place?'

The doctor sighs. 'A modest acolyte.'

Knowing what I now know about Jacobina, I enjoy the man's dilemma.

'Very well.' He smiles with visible effort. 'I know my assistant has mixing of ointment to do.'

She excuses herself and leaves the table, still without meeting my eye. I know it's safer not to risk a look but yearn all the same for a flicker of reassurance, a quick glance to say that she sees how neatly I've freed her to arrange our joint escape. It would tell me that I did not imagine last night.

'While you undress, I must see to a small task.' He leaves the room. Through a window, I watch him go toward the barn, to see that his captives are still secure, I presume. My mind churns. I must make him forget to visit again.

Clothes removed, I snatch a closer look at the book left open on the table. My knees turn to water. I read the title at the top of the page.

'*Homo-vir (Loup-garou).*' Wolf-man.

Werewolf.

My last hope vanishes that Jacobina might be wrong. The doctor lies when he said 'if' my wolf is present. He lies when he refers to me as a colleague. He has already decided what I am. A werewolf. A wolf-man. A specimen to be compared bit by bit with a real wolf. Does he imagine that I share his curiosity? Or am I just a fool in his mind?

I hear him returning and move quickly away from the table.

'What must I do first?' I ask him amiably.

'Begin by measuring the length of your bare foot against the rod.'

I examine the rod in detail before I measure. 'What are these lines.'

'It is laid out in inches and barleycorns.'

I can't think of any further reason to delay. I measure and tell him the figure.

He writes it down in the book. 'Now hold the measuring rod against your lower leg.'

'Why?' I ask.

'Because the limbs of wolves are small and light, compared to the size of their feet. You will see this disproportion when we come to examine the wolf.' The doctor does not object to my question. On the contrary, he sounds delighted to pass on his knowledge. 'And now your upper leg.'

'And I fall where?'

'Somewhere in between.'

'When will that be.' I inquire eagerly. 'That we examine the wolf, that is?'

'When we finish with you.'

I fumble the measuring rod. Drop it, pick it up again.

I keep asking questions as we measure and record my height, my weight, the number and kind of my teeth, and the length of my cock.

'Stick out your tongue!'

'Why?' I ask.

'To determine the colour and the length… dark pink…' He measures it. 'But exceedingly long.' He writes in the book.

He peers into my face. '...eyes are...amber,' he says, writing the colour down. 'With dark brown flecks.'

Wolf-like, I think.

He examines my dusting of body hair much as the priest did. He  draws it onto the outlined human figure in the book.

'What does that patch of hair mean, at the base of my spine?' I ask. The priest had a name for it.

He looks up sharply from his drawing; his enthusiasm for imparting knowledge gives way to a first impatience. 'While I admire your curiosity, it begins to delay our work.'

'Please forgive my ignorance,' I say quickly. 'There's so much for me to learn.'

'The patch of hair at the base of your spine is called a 'wolf patch' by the ignorant...' His voice drips scorn for the ignorant.

I watch the sun drag itself upwards. It is not yet noon. I upset the doctor's pot of oak-gall ink.

'Pray, forgive me!' I look around for a cloth. He snatches it from my hand. Time passes while he wipes up the ink. I get in his way and apologise again. Then he must find more ink. He searches, gives up, grinds some more and re-fills his pot. As he sets the pot back on his table, he looks at me just a little too long. I see the first suspicion in his pale blue eyes.

The noonday bell still does not ring.

'I need your temperature. Open your mouth.' He offers a tube of glass one foot long and as thick as a carrot. He puts it in my mouth. 'Now suck.'

By crossing my eyes, I see a thick central column of silver mercury the diameter of a woman's little finger. A question comes to me. 'What is temperature measured in?' I will ask.

While I suck, he loops string around my skull and lays it out against the measure. He writes the figure in the book. He measures my ears and writes more figures.

My being is taking shape on that page. In spite of my fear, curiosity nudges at me. In other circumstances, I would have liked to learn all there is to know.

A bell begins to ring in a minor key, at last. But it is very far away, faint across the fields. The doctor works on as if he does not hear it. No bell rings on his estate. No one brings food.

I take the tube of glass from my mouth. 'Do you not stop to eat?'

'I do not feel hunger when I work.'

'May I beg some food?'

He throws down his pen. 'If you must!' He goes to the door and shouts, 'Jacobina! He is hungry! And I might as well have some food too.' He thrusts the glass tube back into my mouth. 'We must begin again. This time, do not remove it until I tell you.' He looks towards the stable but stays where he is, perhaps because he does not trust me not to remove the glass tube again.

With it firmly between my lips, I quickly pull on my breeches.

Jacobina brings a tray with a jug of ale, three mugs, freshly baked  bread, a potato and onion stew, dates, and dried meats. She lays out plates among the papers.

The doctor withdraws the glass tube from my mouth.

'Could you not give the doctor one of your sleeping draughts?' I murmur to her while he is writing down whatever he reads from the thick column of mercury.

She seems to ignore me. But as the doctor rummages in a cupboard on the far side of the hall, she murmurs back, 'Watch. Observe for yourself why not.'

He returns from the cupboard with two pistols, which he lays on the table. He raises his brows at Jacobina.

She takes the third mug from the tray, pours from the jug and swallows several mouthfuls of ale. She eats two large spoons of stew, a piece of bread. The doctor points at a random slice of dried meat and a date. She eats them. When she is done, they wait in silence for several moments.

At last he nods. She makes an ironic half-curtsy and leaves.

As hungry as I am, the thought of drugs in the food now makes me ill. I remind myself: I saw Jacobina eat and drink. I chew and chew. Finally swallow. Even so, I manage only four spoons of the potato stew, two bites of bread and a half mug of ale. No dates or meat.

*I am so eager to begin again…I mistook the habit of eating for appetite…*

I rehearse possible reasons for my loss of hunger, but he doesn't ask. He watches impatiently as if counting every move of my jaw.

'If you have satisfied your supposed appetite, can we begin measuring the wolf? We should have begun this morning! You may finish dressing.' He picks up his book, pen and the pistols as he waits. Jacobina returns to clear the food.

I put on the rest of my clothes and follow the doctor from the great hall into what must once have been the chief parlour, a chamber for receiving friends more intimately than in the great hall. It would once have been a pleasant room furnished with chairs and a small table for informal conversation. Painted animals peer down at us from the ceiling. The top half of the walls is lined with leather panels of painted flowers and fruits. Where the fireplace in the great hall could stable a horse, this one would house no more than two goats or a few hens. Something the colour of dried blood is splattered over two faded vases of painted tulips. A feral smell hangs in the air as if the room were crowded by dogs that have rolled in something rotten. The wolf is already there. It bares its teeth when we enter and backs into the farthest corner of a cage smaller than the one in the barn, rumbling in its throat.

The doctor throws it a piece of meat from a plate on the table.

The wolf stops growling and eyes the meat.

I note for the first time that it has expressive, almost human brows that seem to signal its thoughts. Watching it recoil from the meat, looking puzzled, I imagine it thinking:

*Smells wrong. Heavy, sweet. Like rotting leaves. Sniff again. Not rotten. I can eat rotten. Never smelled meat like this before.*

Then it sniffs the meat again. Hunger and caution war in its eyes.

*But there is also rich blood and fresh juice. Dead sheep. The end of the bone gleams smooth and shiny. Round and glistening, it draws my eyes. I can't look away. My empty stomach clings to my spine. It wants to fill and sag as if it will drag on the ground and pull me down into sleep.*

*The meat will fill it, but the meat smells wrong. I smell the man's hands on it, and other hands, the ones that throw my food into the other cage. A puzzling smell, a little like a woman and a little like a man. I have not yet smelled her bleed. I have not yet smelled him aroused by a female.*

A long black tongue snakes out between its teeth and licks the lower jaw. The eyes grow speculative.

Don't eat it! I want to shout.

The doctor now carries the pistols warily.

The wolf stands over the meat. I watch it eye the tempting morsel.

> *It is right here, close to my mouth. I lick it. Lick it again. I can't help myself. I seize it in my teeth and tear. I swallow the chunks fast so I don't taste the sweetness and rotting leaves.*

It gulps down the rest of the meat.

I drop onto my heels to stare into the wolf's cage. I meet its eyes and try to send it my thoughts along our locked eyebeams.

The wolf stares back but remains resolutely of this world, a mere animal, nothing like my demon wolf. It cleans its jaws with a final lick and pushes an inquisitive muzzle through the bars.

Its gamey smell suddenly brings back the dog that was my friend, long ago, in that other place, where I lived with my grandmother beside the canal in Amsterdam. When I was just a handsome boy who sang for whores and their marks in inns and let them rumple my curls while

I collected my coins. Before my demon wolf invaded me and changed my life beyond all understanding.

I exhale gently, as I had done to tell my dog friend what I had last eaten. The wolf sniffs with interest then backs away on wobbling legs as the drug in the meat takes effect. It collapses in a heap of rusty fur. I hear it snore.

I watch the doctor lay the pistols down on a chair on the far side of the room. He would reach the pistols before I did.

He unlocks the cage cautiously. The wolf continues to snore. I keep up my pose as an eager, innocent student.

Together we haul the beast out onto the parlour floor. I measure and call out figures; the doctor writes them in his book: length of leg, diameter of ankles, waist and knees, length of tail. I remember the morning's measurements of me. We map the wolf's ears and structure of shoulders and hips. Standing on its long, slim hind legs, the wolf would be as tall as I am, while its footpads, as large as my fists, suggest an even larger beast.

I make pain and exhaustion my excuse for slow movements as we turn the great beast onto its back and lift the black lips to count, recount, and record the number and shape of the teeth that could have cracked off both our wrists. The wolf snores faintly through all these manipulations.

We roll the beast onto its belly again so that the long blunt muzzle ridged with rust-coloured fur rests on its huge white forepaws. The doctor takes the pistols from the chair, sits by the head, sets the pistols on the floor beside him and begins to sketch the colour of the markings.

I glance at the guns – out of my reach – and then at the window. The sun at last turns orange and begins to set. I want to hang on it to pull it faster towards the horizon.

I watch the doctor work his way down the wolf's body noting the markings of its pelt. The light is now going fast.

He reaches the tail. He lays down his pen. He shakes sand from a shaker onto his drawings then blows it carefully away. He glances at the window. We lock the wolf back in the cage. The doctor picks up the pistols again.

I'm not certain now whether they are meant to protect him against the wolf or against me.

'We're done for today?' I ask as we return to the great hall.

'The light is almost gone, but we can still see well enough for one last investigation.' He tucks the pistols in his belt. I don't know whether I have fooled him or not.

'We must examine your inner pelt. If you are a true werewolf, you are *versipillus*.' He opens his chest of knives. 'That is to say, you have fur beneath your skin, even when you appear to be a man. Your true nature will hide but not disappear.' He selects a scalpel. 'In spite of my reluctance to believe them, I have heard of werewolf attacks reliably reported in Italy and France.'

He turns to me. 'We must now look under your skin.'

Fur under my skin might explain the sensation of heat, but I have failed to stop the cutting.

'Why?' My mouth is dry. 'Why look?' I think about my chances if I try to grab a pistol.

The doctor forces himself to be patient. 'A werewolf is said to be a *versipillus,* a turn-pelt, wearing its fur inside,' he repeats. 'We must look for the fur under your skin.'

Now the flaying begins.

He takes my arm firmly and leads me to the window. He turns over my hands one at a time, peering closely at the insides of my wrists. 'We will test a hypothesis...'

'"Hypothesis"?' I echo. 'I don't quite understand.' The man's touch makes me sick. Is this the moment when I stop pretending?

He sighs impatiently. 'It's Greek. A hypothesis is a theory to be proved or disproved by observed fact. Not a mere intellectual game like the so-called "Ancient Authorities" played, only to amuse themselves.'

I nod to keep him talking.

'We, who lead the way in the New Philosophy...' He cannot help preening a little. '...are fearless in refusing to swallow myth and theories born more than eight hundred years ago.'

I nod.

'No matter that the Church calls us heretics to question God's perfect universe...'

I nod again. My left hand is in his. My eyes are on the guns in his belt.

'...we test a proposition - always test – with our own eyes. Conclusions are to be trusted only if they grow from observed fact.'

'What is the hypothesis that we must test?' I use as many words as I can. Dusk is falling. How dark must it grow before he stops? My hand jumps in his grasp.

Impatiently, the doctor says, 'That you are a true *versipillus*. A werewolf. We find fur beneath your skin. It would be a triumph for the New Learning if I could be the first to examine a werewolf scientifically.' He tightens his grasp on my hand.

And you became the Praelector of Anatomy at Padua, I think. I glance again at the window. Almost dark.

He follows my eyes. 'Don't fear. Candlelight will tell us all we need to know.' He gives me an amused look. 'The area to be examined is small, a square inch or so. We do have time for this final investigation…if it still interests you.'

Candlelight.

But only a square inch.

However much I delay, I cannot stop what is going to happen. Is he now toying with me?

And I have come so close to achieving what I set out to do. Others will suffer too if I flinch now.

'How..?' I begin through stiff lips. I can't think of a question. I can no longer remember how an eager, interested face feels. He must feel the deep shudders shaking my body.

'No more questions. Even with a candle to help us, we must proceed.' He presses down on my skin with his thumbs and bends close to study the veins. Then he looks deep into my eyes. 'Now we come to the first difficult moment in our shared project. Will you permit me to look beneath your skin?'

Small. He said that the area to be examined was small. 'I must learn the truth.' I manage to get the words out.

'I believe that you mean what you say! You surpass my expectations,' he says without a whiff of irony. 'You choose as I would in your place. Not many would.' He seems to mean it as a compliment.

I won't break my cover yet.

He lights a candle with a lens attached to the candlestick to focus the light. Then he asks me to rub a dark brown sticky ointment onto the skin of my left arm.

'Just here?' I ask. I can barely speak. The ointment stinks of damp books and burning leather like the salve that Jacobina used to soothe my back. My left wrist and right fingertips go numb.

He picks up his small gleaming steel blade. 'Can you feel this?' He pricks with the point.

I feel pressure on my skin but no pain.

'How great is your thirst for self-knowledge? Will you watch or avert your eyes?'

He seeks to control me, I think. I must not give way to his control. 'My curiosity is even stronger than my stomach.'

He holds my arm in the halo of candlelight. I feel pressure and a faint sting. The first opening of my flesh. A short red line wells up on my skin. A trickle of warmth as blood runs around my wrist. I smell a coppery metallic tang.

He makes a small second cut at right angles to the first, as if beginning to draw a square. Gently, he prises up the small pointed flap of skin. I see only white-spotted red flesh before the blood wells up and drowns it.

No fur.

The doctor wipes my arm with a square of clean linen and peers through a lens from his instrument chest. He wipes and peers again. He shakes his head.

'I'm not a werewolf!' I feel a rush of ill-timed joy. I am not a werewolf. Kat was right.

'Not so fast! I have seen pictures drawn by supposed eye-witnesses showing werewolves with the head and body of a wolf but human limbs.'

I think of the woodcut on the placard in Cambridge.

'We must therefore also look under the skin of your back. Would you be kind enough…?' He offers the ointment pot again. 'If my fingers are numb, I won't be able to handle the knife.'

To turn my back takes all my will. I think hard of the others – Jacobina, Butters, Dob, Olivia – and their preparations to escape.

Again I feel the pressure of the knife and the trickling heat.

'No fur.' He sounds disappointed.

'I am not a werewolf, after all!'

'The absence of fur suggests the negative. I must look under my own skin, to compare as a control.' He has me apply the salve to his left forearm. He makes the same cuts in his own skin.

'The same as yours.' He sounds both thoughtful and disappointed.

By the time he dresses both our wounds, the light has gone completely. 'We'll stop there for today. Short of what I had hoped but a good day nonetheless.'

I light tallow candles on the table where we will eat. Meanwhile the doctor puts the pistols back in the cupboard. He pours two mugs of the ale left from the midday dinner.

'A good day, if not long enough for greedy curiosity.' The doctor raises his mug to me.

Testing me? 'Not long enough,' I agree, hoisting my mug in return but not drinking yet. I find it suddenly easy to smile. I feel drunk without the help of ale. I survived the day. I succeeded. The doctor had not revisited the barn. I had left Jacobina free to prepare the night's escape. All is now in her strong hands. I have only to wait for her instructions.

She brings a plate of dates, eats the one he points out, waits as before and leaves when he nods. I sniff at them behind the doctor's back but find nothing wrong in their smell.

I am ravenously hungry though wary of eating or drinking. I want to leap in the air, turn somersaults, slide down the bannister of the great staircase. I pace to wear off my exhilaration. I sniff the sheep smell from the tallow candles with pleasure. Whatever I might be and whatever the doctor might mutter about positives and negatives, I am not a werewolf. I will think about the disappearance of Alice Brinkley later. Tonight I will rejoice that I am not a proven werewolf. Tonight I will rejoice that I have survived.

'Tomorrow, my friend, we shall learn together what no man yet knows.' He drinks. He helps himself to the plate of dates. He eats one. Then, remembering civility, he offers the dates to me with suppressed amusement and a hint of challenge in his eye. They're safe, says his look. Watch. He eats another.

I watch him closely, scarcely listening. The next day no longer concerns me. I will be gone. I watch him swallow – no trick that I can detect – with either ale or date. My stomach hurts with hunger. I look longingly at my full mug on the table. My throat is dry.

He drinks again. 'We shall learn where the true nature of a human lies in the body. The soul, if you will. And show that it cannot be found in a beast...Sit! Sit!' He seems really to swallow his ale. He eats another date.

I sit. I can think of no civil way to refuse either ale or dates without betraying myself. I drink and eat a date.

He settles happily back in his high-backed chair-of-grace. 'Tomorrow, we will get to the heart of the matter. To the soul.' He lifts his mug again. 'To my partner in exploration. To human curiosity that will answer all things. To the New Philosophy that will unseat the ignorance of the Ancients!'

The world lurches.

'Sleep well,' he says.

I yawn. A sweet silky sleep reaches for me. I sink to the floor, slow and heavy.

Slowly drifting into a cloud.

I struggle to sit up...grope for thought.

The doctor had shared the ale, eaten dates. I had seen Jacobina taste one.

The dates! As dark as charred wood, and sticky. Strong-smelling. Easy to dose a chosen few. I tried remember whether he had turned the plate when offering me one, but my mind is already forgetting...

You gullible fool!

I did not fool him for a moment.

Teeth clenched, braced upright against a table leg, I fight the drug. I know that my life has suddenly grown very short.

Another moment passes. And another. I am counting my life down to nothing...must not waste one second of it in sleep, in death's shadow. In a half-dream, my ribcage swings open like a pair of cathedral doors. My exposed heart, naked and indecent, tries to tear itself free and escape but is tied in place by slimy blue and white strings. Whatever was in the dates is stronger than my will. I sleep.

# 13

I feel a moment of child-terror. Strange bed. Strange room. My mouth feels like an old owl's nest. My head aches. A painted hare peers down at me. I see faded painted tulips. I'm back in the parlour. It's day again.

I'm still in the doctor's house.

The escape was planned for last night.

I lie spread-eagled naked on a table. My arms and feet are securely tied with rope to the four legs.

I turn my head. The wolf lies on a second table, stretched out on its back as I am, legs tied to each corner, the skin of its belly slung like a hammock below heaving ribs. Beyond it, stands the empty cage. A box of fresh sawdust sits between the two tables.

My head falls back. Jacobina let me distract the doctor so that she and the others could prepare for escape. She drugged the dates. She had lied to me with her talk of flames and guiding me. She and the other 'specimens' fled in the night.

I am alone again, abandoned by my new 'friends'. I am a blemish on the Universe, a treason against Nature.

Alone except for the wolf – and I'm not certain of our relationship.

'Good morrow,' the doctor says cheerfully as he enters, bringing a waft of civet and lavender. 'I trust you slept soundly.' He sets his clinking instrument case on a small table near the tied-down wolf. He goes back and locks the parlour door.

The door key goes into the right-hand pocket of his breeches, under the white butcher's apron he wears. Knowing where the key is does me no good, however, if I can't move. I note that the doctor has left off his robes and is in shirtsleeves.

Shirt is easily washed, my Reason says.

'Can't you trust me? Did you need to use a conjuror's trick on me?' I demand. My eyes run over him again – two pistols are visible.

The doctor smiles. 'Blame yourself.' He begins to set out his knives on the small table. I hear the chink of blades and the wooden clunk of a mallet. 'As eager as you appeared yesterday, I noticed a slight reluctance in you at times, which led me to fear you might flinch at our final voyage of discovery.' He wags his head ruefully. 'In your place, even I might hesitate. I have merely helped you remain true to your claimed curiosity. Tied you to resist your own weakness, like Odysseus tied to the mast at the song of the Sirens.' With a scoop like one for measuring grain, he sprinkles a thick layer of sawdust below my table.

'I swear I will not flinch! Free me! I want only to learn!'

'Don't fear,' the doctor says kindly. 'I'll explain each new discovery to you until the very last moment that you can understand.'

He opens a jar from his case. 'Trust me. With this numbing ointment and the tincture of opium I'll give you to drink, you'll not feel a thing.' He uses a spatula to spread the ointment thickly on my bare chest. My skin goes numb almost at once.

Helpless rage boils up. The last sleep leaves me. My thoughts feel as sharp as broken glass. He was playing with me the day before, could have used the spatula but enjoyed controlling me. He knew all along that I suspected him, that I only pretended to obey. He knew all along that it was pretence on both sides.

He doesn't know or else doesn't care that the others have escaped. 'I mean to be Praelector of Anatomy at Padua...' I remember the triumph with which he held up the human liver at his demonstration and declared that it had two lobes, not like the five lobes of a dog. I was just another canine – or not. He would earn the position of Praelector by proving, or disproving, that I was a werewolf.

He picks up a knife. In a moment, my flesh would part. The knife will open the gaping hole through which my life will drain away into the sawdust.

'Debate,' Jacobina had said. 'He delights in debate.'

I don't trust her about anything, any more. She is not here because she deceived me, abandoned me after a brief, false taste of fellowship. I think of Kat, out of reach in what now seems a normal world. I am truly alone.

I look at the wolf for inspiration. It gives a keening exhalation.

Trust Jacobina or not, academic debate is the only choice I can think of. I fumble for an idea. 'You said yesterday that you will search today for the place in me where my soul lives. What do you hope to prove if you find it?'

'Whether you are man or beast. Man has a soul; a beast does not.'

'Never?' I ask, still fumbling.

'Never. A beast is a mere machine of flesh and bone.' The doctor cannot hide his pleasure in instruction, even now. 'Only man has a soul, which brings love of art, of learning and of God.'

The wolf begins to struggle against its bonds. It whimpers and starts to give off a strong feral smell.

Keep him talking. The man must not begin to look for my soul or for anything else.

Then I have an idea. 'So, if you find the home of my soul,' I say, 'you will find nothing at all occupying that same place in the wolf?'

He nods approval. 'You understand clearly. If you are human, you have a soul. The wolf, a mere animal, does not.' He selects another blade and weighs it in his hand.

The wolf whines again. Its smell intensifies.

Be my ally, I will it. I am about to ask the impossible of you. I force the appearance of eager enthusiasm. 'I have a contrary hypothesis for you.'

The doctor raises bushy eyebrows in the raddled cherub face. 'You will try to prove me wrong?'

'Yes.'

'And what might your instructive hypothesis be?'

'That the wolf has a soul.'

He snorts in derision. 'Fanciful nonsense.' But he sets down the blade and turns back to me with interest. 'Go on."

I keep my eyes off the set-down blade. 'You said that having art is proof of having a soul.'

'Correct.'

'Is music an art?'

'Of course.'

'I will prove that the wolf has music, and therefore art, and therefore a soul.'

'I defy you to prove any such thing.' His eyes sparkle with challenge.

'I think you fear being proved wrong.' I imitate his smile. 'Give me the rest of the day. I need to make friends with the wolf before I can prove a hypothesis or anything else.'

The doctor hesitates then nods.

I have the rest of the day to prove my nonsensical hypothesis. It is nonsense, of course, but I have made a start, with a relatively clear head. The doctor did as I asked. I am untied and dressed again. In spite of occasional waves of dizziness from the drug, it feels like progress. On the other hand, the doctor is armed with the two pistols.

Before freeing me, he brought a dead chicken and pan of water as I asked. He loosened my bonds then locked himself into the empty cage with his book and pen. He pocketed the cage key in his breeches along with the key to the parlour and has laid the two pistols in easy reach on the floor.

'Don't imagine that I won't shoot you – and the wolf – if you make a move in my direction.' He is as safe from me as if I were in the cage.

I struggle to untie myself the rest of the way, make myself find the patience to pick laboriously at the knots. My clothes are piled in one corner. I put them on.

The wolf begins to pant. A pale amber eye flutters open then closes again. I untie it and lower it to the floor, hindquarters first, then the rusty head. As I heave at the forequarters, wild eyes open and swivel to fix on me.

Help me! I beg silently. I need you as my accomplice, not my enemy. Two against one might win, even with the pistols. The odds should be even more in our favour – I think bitterly of the others who must be well away from the estate by now.

It slides down onto the floor, as flat as a wolf skin rug.

'Do you mean to prove that a hearth rug has art?' The doctor's voice holds cheerful contempt. Nevertheless, he leans forward with curious interest.

'Keep silent unless I give you permission!' I assert my temporary authority. I crouch beside the wolf, remembering how carelessly I handled it the day before.

The wolf raises its head dizzily.

Wake up, brother in trouble. I need your help!

The wolf convulses away from me.

Its black brows knit in a frown. I watch the thoughts behind its eyes, as clear as if the animal could speak.

*I must get to my feet. What is wrong? My legs buckle. I fall. Slowly, leg-by-leg, I find my muscles, heave my forequarters into the air. Brace on my front feet. Wait while the world spins around my head. Now, hindquarters up. Tail too heavy to lift. Ears hang like dead leaves. I must move, must run. Nose is awake. I smell anger and fear, a man. A man afraid means danger.*

I see the wolf look around in confusion. Its lips lift in a half-snarl, ears back, its tail pressed flat against its legs.

> *I don't understand. I was in my cage among the smells of frightened animals that had gone but left their scents behind. I am still in a cage but a different, larger one.*

The wolf staggers to the pan of water and drinks it all. It lies down against the locked parlour door, looking from me to the doctor and back again.

> *There are two men with me. One in my former cage. I smell the stink of his fear but he is beyond my reach. The other sits on the floor not far from me with lowered head and averted eyes, like a pup, afraid in a different way. He does not challenge me. A cleaner smell than the other - but not attacking. With one eye on him, I rise and stagger around the walls of this new cage, measuring them. No room in any direction to stretch into a run. I bump the walls with my shoulder, pretending not to watch him. He does*

*not move. I pause to sniff. A male cat has peed in*
*this corner. I lift my leg and mark over his scent*
*before I continue around the cage. I don't like this*
*new cage, but it is my territory. The man sitting on*
*the floor still does not challenge my rule.*

The wolf trots in circles around the walls, avoiding the
cage from which the doctor watches and makes
occasional notes in his book. I sit without moving on the
floor. The wolf stops once to sniff at me.

The doctor looks genuinely alarmed. 'It will tear you
apart.'

I wait motionless. If the doctor is right, I prefer that
death to dying slice-by-slice under the doctor's knives,
however painlessly.

The wolf moves away. I offer it the chicken with my
foot. 'Come, then. Eat.' I pull my foot back. My
outstretched leg seems a more tempting meal than the
damp, limp-necked hen.

The wolf streaks across the floor, snatches the
chicken, retreats to the far wall and turns its back to eat. I
hear bones crack between its teeth. It looks over its vast

shoulder at me then buries its muzzle in the feathers again.

When it has eaten all of the chicken except for the long wing feathers, the wolf begins to circle the room again. A nose touches my ear from behind. A large russet-streaked head moves into the side of my vision. Slowly, I raise a hand and offer it for examination. The wolf sniffs at my fingers then pushes its long blunt muzzle close to my face. I close my mind to its teeth and make myself sit very still, inhaling and exhaling slowly as the animal tests my breath.

The wolf peels back its black lips and nips my shirtsleeve.

'No!' I exclaim before I can stop myself.

The startled animal shies away. It pauses in the centre of the room and stares into my eyes. Its head is higher than mine and its gaze feels like the pressure of a hand.

I pat the floor as if inviting a dog to play.

The wolf stares at me in astonishment. I pat the floor again. It does not respond but stands staring at me. It walks towards me, stands in front of me for a moment, still staring. It sits, shoulder-to-shoulder. Cautiously, I lay my hand on its nape. A pale amber eye turns my way.

I scratch behind the ears as if the wolf were a huge hound. To my amazement, the animal settles beside me. I continue to scratch. I stroke the rough, rust-grey head, then scratch some more. Filled with a deep, astonishing sense of calm in spite of my circumstances, I begin to hum, a pleasant buzzing in the bones of my face.

'How long will you try to delay the inevitable?' demands the doctor.

'Silence!' I say with authority. 'Or you will be the cause of any delay.'

He settles back inside the safety of the cage.

Now we come to it, I tell the wolf silently.

I hum more loudly. I look at the wolf. Forgive me for rushing you, I think. I know it's day, there's no moon. And I don't know how this will sound.

I begin to sing softly. I stop in surprise. I begin again. I listen to the music I'm making. Dry as my voice is, I am singing again.

The wolf cocks its ears. No doubt it can also hear the drumming of my heart.

My voice climbs step by step. I try to capture the mournful mode of the wolf's howl. The wolf looks away, then straight back at me. It may be embarrassed or confused. I hope it can read my good intent.

Please, I implore silently. I know that it's daylight, and there's no moon, but, please! I sing the climbing scale again, through the stretched eerie notes that had pinned my heart two days before.

The wolf stands up and looks intently into my eyes.

The muscles of its throat quiver. Its throat quivers again. I hear a faint hollow whine.

Please, I beg.

Holding my eyes, the wolf stretches its head forward and makes a hollow trumpet of its muzzle. Its jaw quivers. The quiver becomes a faint howl. The howl grows louder. The fur of its ruff trembles. The wolf raises its head higher and higher as its voice climbs.

My voice begins to climb again. It grows louder as the wolf grows louder. I slide my notes into the gaps in the wolf's song. Our voices intertwine, weaving together.

'Listen!' I whisper to the doctor. Miraculously, in full daylight, the wolf and I are howling together.

Not nonsense after all.

We howl again.

My voice loosens. I adjust my tune to that of the wolf. Our voices climb yet again, entwined in harmony but always on different notes.

The wolf throws back its head farther and farther until the hollowed muzzle points at the sky. Its voice resonates in my body. My own howl vibrates in my chest and throat and scours deep into my belly.

'Listen!' I whisper again in wonder.

Mingled with that of the wolf, my voice slides upward, approaches dangerous disorder, finds order again. Each time we arrive at the top of a climb, our voices come together in a moment of perfection. Then comes a moment of perfect stillness.

Our music runs round the inside of my skull, polishing it smooth and clean. As I look into the animal's eyes and feel my way upwards through our shared music, I forget the doctor, lost in the wonder of this unbelievable song.

The wolf has given me back my voice. I can sing again.

We howl again for the pure pleasure of it. Our shared song is an opening into my profound being. I am a pipe, a conduit. My voice pours out through it. If this is my double nature, I glory in it.

'What do you imagine you proved with that display of beastly noise?'

I look beyond the wolf to see the doctor standing out of the cage, a pistol pointed at my heart.

The wolf stops howling abruptly and watches with pricked ears and great intensity.

'Did you not hear?' I still float in wonder. 'That was music! The wolf has music, after all!'

'I heard no music. Only beastly noise.'

'You are a man of science, but I am a musician. I tell you, that was music! And in the Lydian mode!' I reach to touch the wolf's head, still filled with the unimaginable joy of our shared song.

The pistol shakes with the force of his rage. 'You could have died nobly, as I would have done in your place, while increasing man's knowledge. But you're an ignorant clod after all. Now you'll never know the whole truth about yourself.'

'You are the ignorant clod!' How could the man have listened and not heard? 'That was truth beyond my imagining. And, it seems, beyond your understanding.'

We stand face to face, man against boy.

The doctor's voice is icy. 'To think that I gave you credit for human wits! But, as you see, I command the best Reason of all.' He waves the pistol. 'Please save us both trouble by getting back onto the table. After hearing you howl together, I'm eager to compare your throats.' He raises his voice, unable to hide his fury. 'Back onto the table!'

The wolf growls.

'Steady, boy,' I say soothingly. I'm thinking clearly again. If the wolf attacks, the doctor will shoot it. He must not shoot the wolf. The odds are two to one although the one is armed. The doctor is out of the cage. There must be a way.

The doctor lowers his voice at the wolf's growl, but his intensity still trembles in it. 'Why delay? Sooner or later, you know you must eat or drink and be forced to swallow whatever is in the food I give you. Or else you will weaken past resisting.'

My lips pull back from my teeth. 'You must shoot me first.' All that had happened since arriving in England now boils up in me. This time, there are no footpads. No farmers with guns. No chains. I want to tear out the doctor's throat. I want the wolf's great jaws to crush the skull that holds such remorseless, cruel curiosity. I imagine the wolf's teeth, as long as a man's thumb, tearing into the soft pale flesh and crushing the fingers that turn the keys in locks and press so tenderly on scalpels cutting into flesh.

'Onto the table!' repeats the doctor. I start towards him.

The wolf turns its head towards the door.

The locked door flies open and crashes back against the wall. Butters arcs through the door, hits the floor in a handstand, rebounds, flies through the air again and lands on his feet on the fireplace mantle shelf.

The doctor gapes at the open door behind him. 'How did you get free?'

'You need better locks.' Butters cartwheels along the mantle shelf. 'Yours are too easy to pick.' He bows.

The wolf had raises its rusty muzzle to smell the air. It crouches and takes a stealthy step towards Butters. The moment of near comedy turns dangerous again.

'Leave him, boy!' I shout. But the wolf is not a trained hound. It prepares to leap. I throw myself across the room to stop it.

Before I can reach it, the room fills with a cackling and frantic beating wings. A flock of chickens bumps and ricochets, their terror intensified by the feral smell of the wolf. Black and white feathers float in the air.

I'm dreaming, I think wildly. Where did they come from?

A rooster lands on the doctor's head, loses its balance and flaps to the floor. The wind of its wings fans my hair as I see in the side of my eye, through the melee of flapping birds, the shapes of two young men coming through the door. If those are the doctor's men, I am dead. But I will kill the doctor first.

The birds careen wildly through the air, squawking, 'Death! Death!' The wolf leaps and snatches a screeching hen from the air. It turns with the bird still flapping in its jaws and races past the two men, out through the open door. The Dutch street scum takes me over.

The doctor fires one of the pistols. Butters dives to the floor. A bloody hen falls twitching from the air.

The doctor steadies his other gun, pointing at my head. I catch a hen out of the air and throw it at his face as he fires again. The bullet hits one of the windows.

Butcher's apron protects the doctor's groin, his guns tossed aside, useless until reloaded. In a shower of falling glass, I charge at him.

I kick his knee as he reaches for the dagger he has hidden in his right boot. As he falls, the knife clatters on the floor. I kneel with one knee in his back, ready to break his neck.

'Don't kill him! It's too quick.' The blonde curls have been cropped to below the ear, but I know the face and smell.

'I'm "Jack" just now, not Jacobina. Don't look so astonished...Here's rope.'

I recognise the other youth as Dob.

They are still here.

Ignoring the mayhem around him, Dob scoops up a panic-stricken hen, soothes it under his arm and puts it gently into a basket cage by the door.

The doctor writhes and bucks to throw me off, weeping with pain. I keep my knee in his back while Jack lashes his hands together behind his back then catches the kicking feet and ties them.

Dob catches and quiets another hen as if alone in the room. 'Chook, chook,' he murmurs. 'Come, princess...' He makes soft noises, then begins to hum.

Butters raises his head cautiously from the floor.

I roll the groaning doctor onto his back and get to my feet. 'She...he is right. You've shed too much blood to get off without paying.' I heft the dropped pistol. I look at the heavy knob on the end of the pistol grip.

'Don't kill me!' whimpers the white-faced doctor. 'Man's knowledge still needs my work.'

'Go ahead,' says Butters, standing and brushing off his clothes. 'He meant to murder us. Finish him. Break his skull.'

'Please!' begs the doctor.

I smell urine. He has wet himself.

'Did you show mercy when your "specimens" begged?' I ask. 'Bleed in your turn!' I strike him backhanded across the face with the flat of the gun. The protruding flintlock gouges his cheek.

The doctor screams. A scarlet line of blood runs down his cheek.

'Go fetch the jars!' Jack orders. Dob sets down a hen and runs from  the room.

I wipe the pistol and put it in my belt.

'Now, some of his own medicine.' Jack takes a small stoneware jar and spatula from the leather bag at his waist and prises off the cover. 'Recognise this?' he asks the doctor. 'Wolf's bane and thorn apple, among much else.'

The doctor stares at the brown-grey paste inside the jar. He clamps his lips shut and shakes his head. He tries to sit but falls back again. 'No!' he says through clenched teeth. He shakes his head so violently from side to side that his cheeks wobble.

A spatula, I think. So simple.

'Hold him!' cries Jack.

Butters twists his hands into the man's hair so tightly that the scalp lifts from the skull. I sit on the doctor's chest while Jack raises his bloody upper lip and applies salve thickly with the spatula on his gum.

The doctor's eyes bulge. He pushes at the salve with his tongue. Butters tightens his grip on the doctor's hair. Jack pulls down the man's lower lip and lays a strip of ointment along the lower gum. Then he clamps the man's mouth shut with his hand.

'Hallucinations first, sleep after,' he says. 'A good use for an evil substance. It won't take long to work... but you already know that.'

The doctor groans.

Jack does not remove his clamping hand. 'We won't kill you, much as some of us would like to... show you more compassion than you've ever shown your victims. We don't want your blood on our hands. When the salve wears off, you're free to raise help. We'll leave you tied, of course...Is your mouth going numb yet, by the way?'

Dob returns to the parlour with three jars: a deformed human foetus, a human hand, and the child-like heart. He sets them in a grisly display on the dissecting table where the wolf had been tied.

'We'll leave these to welcome any rescuers.' Jack leans close to the doctor's face. 'When would it have been my turn on the table?' he asks quietly. 'When would you have added my parts to that collection?'

The doctor shuts his eyes. His voice has already begun to grow thick and fade. '...thought you understood wha' we were doing together.'

'Oh, that I did,' says Jack. 'But I didn't care for my part in it.'

'Traitor…' The doctor looks wildly at the specimen jars, then at some invisible terror on the ceiling. He goes limp.

I push him with my foot. 'Gone from this world.' I untie him again and place him on the table where I had been. I stretch him spread-eagled and securely tie his wrists and ankles to the four legs, having first removed his boots. I search his pockets and remove the blade with which he cut me free in the carriage. I take the scabbard from his boot.

'Strip him,' says Butters.

I repress a shiver. 'This will do!' I hold up the blade.

'When he wakes, he can apply pure Reason to his plight,' says Jack. 'Those pickled horrors should see him either hanged for murder or burnt for wizardry.' Jack stares down at the limp form on the table. 'The New Philosophers will disown him if they know how far he takes "observing for himself". And they'll never make him Praelector of Anatomy at Pisa.'

We search his clothes once more, take all keys. I strap the doctor's dagger sheath from his ankle to my own leg.

'Don't ever ask me to do that again.' While Jack and I repack all the doctor's knives in the chest, Butters finishes dusting himself, glaring at us. 'However nicely you ask me to act the fool, that was absolutely the last time! Acrobatics! I think I've torn a muscle in my arm.' He rotates his shoulder.

Jack tests the doctor's ropes one more time. 'He should sleep four or five hours. We have at least that long to get well away.' He takes the wooden chest of knives and leaves the parlour with the doctor sleeping inside on the table. We pass through the hall and into a maze of small corridors and kitchens. I smell the odours of roasting meat and dairy from the apron hanging on a hook we pass in a narrow corridor. Jack opens a door.

'I thought you had all escaped last night!' I still struggle to accept the new reality. We enter the yard behind the house.

Jack looks astonished. 'And leave you behind?'

In the barn, Jack hides the chest of knives in the hayloft. Then he pulls a coat for me and a heavy, woven rush pack basket with leather shoulder straps from under a pile of hay on the barn floor. He begins to help me put the basket on. 'I'm sorry you were dosed so heavily,' he says as he re-buckles one shoulder strap to fit me. 'I couldn't control what the doctor gave you. At least, he didn't kill you!'

Dob ties the sleeping Olivia, out of her cage, to his broad, strong back, her limp legs hooked over his arms, a basket on her back. Jack makes a rueful face. 'A shame to dose her for the escape, but she screams otherwise. And Dob won't leave her.'

'I won't leave the wolf, neither,' I say. And I must leave some sign for Kat that I've been here. If she gets here…if she still wants to.

'We can't bring that beast!' cries Butters. 'It will eat us in our sleep!'

Jack slings the strap of a heavy clinking case over one shoulder. 'We've no time to search. It's free. Will have to look after itself.'

'Farmers will shoot it! Or it will starve. It's not used to feeding itself.' I shrug my pack basket back onto the barn floor.

'We can't afford to wait!'

The others start out.

I run to look for the wolf. It is not in the hen house seeking another meal nor the deserted dairy house that smells of mould and sour milk. I scan the fields – no sign of the rusty head and blunt muzzle that sang with me. I search the shadows under garden hedges where an animal might hide. I go into the house. As I look under beds and behind doors, a growing heaviness weighs me down. The wolf has gone, just as I am beginning to accept our bond.

Then I hear a creak from behind the closed door of a little closet where grooms would once have slept on mattresses on the floor.

I fling open the door, not stopping to think how the wolf could have closed it.

'Stay away from me! All of you!' The elderly maidservant scrabbles away from me across the floor, gibbering in terror. 'Avaunt! Godamercy! God save me!' Apron over her eyes, she crosses herself and tries to press herself through the far wall.

'I won't harm you, Mistress,' I say. 'I'm seeking…'

She hunches down, drops the apron, eyes squeezed tightly shut. She claps her hands over her ears. 'Words of the devil! Words of the devil! I've just seen what you all get up to! Devils! Sons of Beelzebub! Beasts! Unnatural fiends! "Easy work," my son-in-law said. "Take the post, mother. Good wages." But he didn't know...'

'Mistress, you must leave here,' I say gently. 'Is there anyone close by who will take you in? Your son-in-law, perhaps?' I step towards her to try to lead her out.

Her eyes open a crack. She screams and flaps her arms at me. 'Werewolf! Don't touch me! Don't put me in a jar! I saw the jars! Wizards, all of you!'

I raise my hands in defeat. 'I'll leave the doors open.' She will call the nearest watch when she calms down enough. So much for our four or five hour head start. I must leave the wolf if I want to escape with the others, but it feels like leaving part of me behind.

Through a window I see the rest already disappearing at a run through an orchard. Jack leads on long, strong legs in men's breeches, one arm holding close the case of medicines slung on a strap over one shoulder. Loping behind him, Dob carries the sleeping Olivia on his back. Butters scrambles third in a lop-sided run, a bundle under each arm.

I run back to the barn, struggle into my pack and set off after them.

# 14

Jack stops running at a small door in the far wall of the estate. He holds up a heavy iron key. The key turns easily, the lock already oiled. Jack smiles at the rest of us. 'Oh, yes. While you've been doubting me, I've been preparing to escape. Including stealing this key two nights ago when the doctor finally slept.'

We step through the gate out of the estate like people stepping from darkness into the light, a little dazed by our freedom. Jack relocks the gate behind us and shifts the strap of his bulky medicine case. He flings the key into the trees. Then he faces us and draws a deep breath.

'We must now decide – travel together or travel apart. Reason says, travel apart. We will draw more attention as a group than if we separate... go our own ways.' He looks each of us in the eye. 'We now return to the very real dangers of a world that rejected us in the first place. All face different threats... different fears.'

Butters glares at him, still breathing hard from our run. 'I'd best go my own way then, being the most conspicuous. Don't want to cause difficulty.' The little man is older even than I thought, the oldest among us. The afternoon sun exposes his wrinkles and grey hair.

Dob takes a firmer grip on Olivia's legs. He seems barely winded by our run in spite of her weight and whatever is in the basket. 'We two will go together. Look for a farn.'

'A farm?' Jack asks. 'For both of you?'

Dob nods with determination. 'I like to work with aninals. She'll...' He jerks his chin at the girl on his back. 'Won't get...' He stops in frustration, trying to find the easiest words to say. 'Not a changeling... gets angry!'

I know what is really being asked. I clench my fists in indecision. As long as I do not turn wolf, stay away from Cambridge, avoid ballad-singers and no one recognises me as a fugitive child-killer, I can pass as an ordinary youth. On my own, I stand a reasonable chance of reaching Seabright Hall, if I can find it. Seabright Hall might be isolated enough to hide me. Jack is right about drawing attention. Reason tells me to head for the place alone. Or with Jack, who also hides a double nature from the casual eye. We can take shelter, for a time at least, while I decide what to do next.

214

Seen through the eyes of the world, the rest are hard to miss: a dwarf, or imp as the superstitious would call him; a changeling who reveals her strangeness as soon as you try to speak to her; and a so-called 'son of the devil' with the split muzzle of a hare.

Except for Olivia, they are all looking at me.

I look back with changed, new eyes.

My new eyes see a woman-man in a single body, who is mistress, or master (take your choice) of dreams, of cures and of killing. My new eyes see a brave, if tetchy, little man who has flown through the air to save my life. They see a youth with a split muzzle disguising him as a beast who is, in truth, a Master of Beasts with the power to quiet and soothe. He also saved my life. He carries on his back his princess, under an evil spell, whose language he seems to speak.

And then there's me – tall and dark and with wolf-amber eyes, who has just rediscovered the joy of singing with a real wolf while still fearing his internal soul-wolf.

They risked their lives to save mine. All of us are so-called 'treasons against nature'. I am one of them. We have power in our union. Are all of us not standing here, free?

Like Kat, they saved my life. I wish she was here, but Kat is not for the likes of me. She belongs in the ordinary world that I have left behind, like it or not. I imagine bidding these people farewell and setting off alone. Though I've known them such a short time, I can't do it. I am one of them. We belong together – a fellowship of the different.

I unclench my fists. 'Come with me to my family's abandoned estate in Lincolnshire. If we can find it.' I hear the release of held breaths.

'Anywhere will suit me so long as there's no need to entertain by playing the fool, though that's all they think I can do.' Butters bends to rub one knee. 'I'm done with capering. Too old for it.'

Dob takes a new grip on the legs of the drowsy girl on his back. 'I can help you work on the eshtate.'

'Can't promise safety,' I warn. They must make their decision with full knowledge of the risks they run. 'I am pursued for killing a child...'

'Did you do it?' Butters interrupts.

'I'm not sure.' I raise my arms helplessly and let them fall. 'I can't promise anything. A house like the one which has been described to me may not have stood empty all these years. I may have to convince whoever is living there that it belongs to me.'

Butters gives me a long searching look. Then he nods.

Dob nods.

The brilliance of Jack's smile warms me. 'We are agreed, I think, to come with you, to find Seabright Hall, if you truly want us.'

Butters shrugs. 'Whatever your odds, they sound as good as any others on offer.'

An emotion I can't name thickens my throat and makes speaking dangerous.

There is general throat-clearing as relief hits us.

'I think that I've just understood that I might be free.' Butters blows his nose. 'Do you know where in Lincolnshire you're taking us?'

'More or less,' I say.

But I've begun with honesty, and it feels good. '...No, not really,' I admit. I suddenly realise that I have no idea where I am now. I do not know how I got from Dover to Grillet's orchard, nor where Cambridge is in relation to where I want to go. Nor where the doctor took me. 'All I know is that it's where the land meets the sea beyond The

Wash, a half day's ride from Boston. And that I'll see the estate from the sea wall, which I assume is like a Dutch dike...whichever way Lincolnshire lies,' I mutter, shamefaced.

Butters glances at the setting sun. 'For my sins, I once played at fairs in those parts.' He turns his left shoulder on the sun and points north, away from the doctor's estate. 'I think Lincolnshire is that way.'

We set off with the setting sun behind our left shoulders, towards the cover of some trees and, with luck, Seabright Hall. I look back at the high stone wall behind us.

'If it wants to find you, it will,' says Jack.

Though he has agreed to come to Lincolnshire, Butters nevertheless walks at a distance from me, watching me in sidelong glances.

# 15

*Chit-chit-chit!* A robin shouts a warning as we trudge past. *Intruders! Danger!*

'If we are to stay together, we must travel by night,' Jack says, 'beginning tonight.'

Butters groans. I feel like doing the same. I hear the blood rushing in my ears and the panting of Butters.

Olivia gives a gentle snore then coughs. A vast silence poised between day and night is broken only by these sounds, the occasional bird, the faint velvety brushing of grass against our legs and the stumbling tread of our feet.

The sun drops out of sight behind us through trees, taking with it our compass. The light under the trees fades to blue shadows. Then a first night frog begins to peep. A chorus swells behind it: soprano, tenor croak,  and a steady, deep bass boom.

Butters limps to a stop. 'Those frogs mean water. If we keep going in the dark, we'll fall in and drown!'

Dogs bark faintly in the distance.

I exchange glances with Jack. I'm almost too tired to get the words out. 'Just guard dogs, I think. Spreading evening news from farm to farm.'

Dob nods his agreement.

'I think we're far enough from the doctor's estate to pause for a bit.' Jack bites his lower lip in thought; the gesture makes me think of Jacobina. 'This wood gives us cover to rest and eat. Cook this, if we can.'

He pulls a limp hen from the sack that balances his heavy chest of clinking bottles. 'Seemed a waste to leave them all behind.'

'And I know how to make a hidden fire that won't give us away.' Butters miraculously recovers strength. He studies the ground. 'There.' He squats and begins to remove the turf, which he sets aside.

Dob unties Olivia from his back and lowers her gently to the ground. She begins to wake. Jack opens his medicine chest to dose her again. But Dob strokes her hand just as he soothed the frightened hens. 'Hush. Hush. I'll look after you now,' he says in his breathy, nasal voice. 'No fear. Hush.' He hums tunelessly.

Jack watches her for a moment. Then, he takes a bread loaf from his sack and begins to tear it. He offers a piece to Olivia.

She seizes it and stuffs it into her mouth.

'No cage,' murmurs Dob. 'Not ever again.'

She gives him a long level look. Then she picks crumbs from her skirt and eats them.

Jack and I exchange another look, tentative relief this time.

While Butters scrapes out a small pit in the earth, Jack guts the hen and buries the entrails. Then he coats it in mud, feathers and all.

There is a rustle in the bushes.

Jack grabs the knife used on the chicken. I sniff the air and put out a calming hand. I feel quiet joy. 'You found us.'

The wolf slinks out of cover, creeping close to the ground. With a faint whine, it lies down beside me, between me and Olivia.

Butters eyes it warily, but it ignores him now, filled as it is with hen. 'Your wolf was raised in a menagerie...won't know how to hunt,' he observes. He has laid dry wood in the hole he has dug. One eye still on the wolf, he makes a small nest of dry twigs and dead leaves on the wood in the pit.

'It knows well enough how to track,' I retort. 'I've been watching but never spied it. It must have leapt over the wall.' The wolf's ears twitch, then it settles its muzzle on its front paws.

Olivia strokes the large shoulder of the wolf, then leans across it to stroke me in the same place. She leans back, seeming satisfied by whatever she has learned. I drop my head onto my knees.

In the darkness of my head, Kat again strokes my face. Her hand is warm. My belly clenches. That's gone, I tell myself. She's not for you. But my belly remains clenched.

Butters strikes sparks with a flint and steel which he takes from his pocket. He nurses the  sparks. The dry tinder catches and flares. He blows gently. Olivia suddenly speaks. 'Fifty fingers.'

Butters lifts his head in astonishment from his tiny new-born fire.

All our heads turn to her. No one dares say a word.
'Fifty toes.'

'Yes,' Dob agrees finally. 'Five people.'

'Twenty toes. One tail,' she adds.

'Wolf,' I say.

Olivia nods and returns to her private thoughts. The rest of us exchange glances. Her first words. After a searching look at Dob, Jack and me, Butters returns to his fire.

We don't dare to speak about her in front of her. She is clearly more aware of us and understands us better than we had thought. Our eyes keep turning to her: a changeling, awake, an unknown factor in our flight.

Jack lays the mud-cased hen on the fire and pulls burning embers over it.

Without warning, Olivia reaches curiously to touch the fire. Dob grabs her hand. 'No! It will hurt you!'

Her body goes rigid. She stares at his hand gripping hers, draws a breath and screams. Jack reaches for his case and uncorks a bottle.

Dob waves him away. Olivia screams again. Dob strokes her as he did the hens. Hums. She looks at him. Draws a breath to scream again.

'Like this.' Dob lifts Olivia's hand gently to the warmth. 'Not too close. Now, it's good.' She looks at the fire and back at Dob. Slowly, her body softens. She lets out her breath.

Jack lifts his head, listening. I also listen for pursuers drawn by her screams.

Cautiously, Dob releases her hand. She continues to hold it out to the fire. She does not try again to touch the flames.

'Nothing,' murmurs Jack. 'Her screams may have been mistaken for an owl or fox.'

As I stare at Olivia's hand, the flames jump like the torch in Grillet's barn and the back-lit priest. I shut my eyes. The flames still jump hot and red against my lids. The world begins to slide and slither.

I bury my head on my knees. 'My demon wolf may be coming! Don't let it hurt you! Kill me first!'

A hand touches my shoulder. 'Let it come. I will keep you safe. ' Jack's voice.

The bubble of horror rises up from under my breastbone and lodges in my throat. A hand on my shoulder holds me steady. Every snap of the fire cuts like broken glass. The rustle of tree leaves deafens me. The smell of smoke fills my nose and mouth. I taste blood and lemons.

The hand on my shoulder anchors me.

'It passed the last time,' says a calm voice. 'It will pass again.'

Chaos fills my head. I no longer know who I am. The beast presses into my head and twines into my muscles. It pulls at the shape of my skull, changing the set of my face. I pull at my clothes that are suddenly too hot against my skin. I try to clamber to my feet to run. A weight on my shoulder stops me. The beast throws back its head and wails in despair.

The hand on my shoulder becomes the roots of a giant tree, holding me steady on the earth. 'You are not fleeing death this time. It's safe. They don't pursue us yet. And we wait for the chicken to cook.'

Slowly, the beast begins to retreat. As it goes, sleep rushes into the space it leaves. My head drops. I fight to stay awake. Hands turn me gently and lay me on the ground. A cloak covers me. 'You are among friends.'

I feel the warm body of the wolf stretched out beside me.

When I wake a little later, Jack sits near me. The flames have died to red coals beneath a coat of grey ash. Dob and Butters doze in exhaustion, wrapped in their cloaks. Butters snorts and twitches restlessly. Dob breathes with a low steady sound like the rush of a tiny stream. Olivia lies curled tightly in a grassy nest, almost invisible, her cloak pulled tightly over her head.

'Welcome back,' says Jack. 'You had four witnesses before the others fell asleep. You did not turn into a wolf or any other beast.'

'And you may believe that I was wary,' Butters's voice croaks from the heap of his cloak. 'It's bad enough fearing your cursed pet.'

'You trembled and moaned,' says Jack. 'Bared your teeth and wailed, tore at your clothes, but you did not attack anyone – nor even threaten to.'

'I'm a reliable witness,' says Butters from his cloak.

'And I,' echoes Dob from his cloak. 'And – good news – Olivia ignored you.'

'Your real wolf was concerned about you, but it fell asleep when you did,' adds Jack.

'I did not turn wolf?' I'm dazed with sleep. 'I did not attack anyone?' I sit up.

'You did no harm to anyone, nor even threaten to do it.'

Dob and Butters nod.

They're mistaken. I know it. I felt the beast invade me. It is too dark to see. They could all be wrong. My demon beast must not have been hungry.

The real wolf still lies beside me, awake now. I sink my hand into its warm fur. Delicate ribs rise and fall under my fingers. My supposed other self looks deep into my eyes, then drops its muzzle onto its forepaws and sighs.

What am I feeling? Beyond all doubt, something invades me.

Jack stoops and delicately fingers my left temple. 'That blow those footpads gave your head may have let in a soul-wolf. I've seen it happen before and heard of still more cases.'

A flea deep in the wolf's pelt tickles my fingertip. As the wolf breathes in and out, the hairs of its fur slide over each other with a quiet murmur very like that of the sea. I listen to the reeds of the nearby swamp clattering against each other.

'But I hear and smell too much! Like a dog or wolf, not a man.'

'Can you see this new difference as a gift, not a curse?' With a stick, Jack rakes the mud-coated chicken from the glowing coals. 'Accept the gifts and live with the dangers.' He cracks open the mud overcoat, releasing a delicious smell of roast chicken. 'As I do...though none of us underestimates the dangers of fear and ignorance.'

'How can the loss of myself to an invading wolf-like being – soul-wolf or not – bring me gifts?' Then I remember my joy when singing with the wolf and the opening of my throat that let my voice rise up, entwined with the real wolf's voice, pure and direct, from the centre of my being. Without my invading wolf, I would never have experienced that joy.

'But Alice Brinkley...' Her disappearance must still be explained. I swallow the rest of my words. I have enough to think about.

We sit around the little fire under the trees. The feathers of the hen come away with the baked mud shell. Jack pulls off a steaming leg and hands it to Olivia. While the wolf watches intently, he tears off pieces for the rest of us. We toss the hot chicken from hand to hand. I blow on some chicken to cool it and offer it to the wolf.

Finally, it seems to say with every muscle in its body. It takes the meat from my fingers with delicate precision. I watch it gulp down the chicken. Unable to wait, we stuff the meat into our mouths and suck in cooling breaths as we chew.

'Whether I turn dangerous beast, or not,' I say. '...people still fear me and want to kill me. They still believe I killed and ate a child.'

'Not everyone is filled with fear.' Jack waves around the circle of shadowy chewing faces. 'Accept our acceptance.' He pulls a bite off and swallows. 'Don't push us away. We'll help – do our best to keep you away from the people who are dangerous.'

Sick regret rushes at me like fast-moving tide across a flat beach. Kat did not fear me either. I can still feel her cheek against my bare chest and her hair tickling my mouth as we huddle under the horse blanket.

I pushed her away for her own good. I still believe it. But I can't help imagining her here, resting now under the same cloak for warmth, leaning against me.

The wolf stiffens suddenly under my hand. It lifts its head and pricks its ears. It stands and listens intently, its muzzle pointed to the southeast through the trees. Then I hear what has disturbed it.

The unified baying of hounds. Not estate guard dogs any longer.

I turn my head slightly to gauge their direction and speed. Not coming any closer. 'A dog pack may be gathering at an estate to the southeast of us.'

The wolf growls softly.

Then Jack hears them too and swears. 'At least they waited for your soul-wolf to pass!' He stands up stiffly. '"Gathering," you say? Not pursuing?'

I nod, still listening.

'The men won't want to blunder about in the dark even if the dogs know where they're going.' He wipes his hands on his breeches and kicks earth over the fire, which hisses as the damp puts it out. 'Pursuit will most likely start at first light. But we can't take the chance.'

Butters quickly replaces the stones and grass he has carefully set aside. We snatch up our burdens, stuff our unfinished chicken into pockets and pouches.

Olivia stands. Dob waits. With absolute certainty, she sets off on her own into the darkness along the faint line of a narrow track. She does not look back to see who follows.

Butters studies the darkness under the trees and slightly lighter sky. 'I think she's right, you know. Headed north, the way we want to go.'

In tense silence, we all follow Olivia along the faintly visible line, away from the dogs. Except the wolf, which makes its own way.

The distant barking reverberates in my head. I keep seeing the mastiff, eyeing me, assessing me, looking for the killing grip. My stomach heaves at the remembered sharpness of the dog's bristles in my mouth and warmth of its blood on my chin. I concentrate on where I am putting my feet and wonder what the real wolf would have done.

It takes shape from the shadows ahead of us and bangs in a friendly fashion against my hip before trotting off again. I realise that it has to keep running in wide loops so as not to leave us all far behind. I find the fact comforting that it reappears from time to time, as if checking that I'm still there.

We emerge from the woods. Near the looming sails of a slumbering wind-pump at the top of a rise, Olivia turns left along a crossing track. She seems to be taking us back closer to the dogs. Jack shakes his head and strikes off along the track to the right, followed by Butters. Dob stops. I hesitate.

Olivia keeps walking to the left. Her dark shape is nearly out of sight in the grey pre-dawn light.

'What will you do if she doesn't return?' I ask Dob.

For a moment, I imagine a flash of panic in his face. Then he smiles.

The girl is walking back. Without comment, Dob falls in beside her at the end of the line, following Jack.

After crossing a muddy stream, our new track divides. Jack hesitates then chooses the branch to the left. But this fork dwindles into a skein of tracks that wander at random.

'Aninal tracks,' warns Dob.

The tracks disappear altogether.

Suddenly, we are in a bog. Setting off alarmed quacks and splashes, we fight for balance. Our feet slip off solid hummocks and sink deep into mud. Our shoes soon grow soaked. We have plough-horse hoofs of mud. The wolf has disappeared, keeping its feet dry on higher ground, no doubt.

Together, the shapes of Dob and Olivia overtake the rest of us. They leap from hummock to hummock, vanishing ahead into the darkness. We splash after them.

'Help me!' cries Butters somewhere on my left. 'I'm sinking too deep!'

'You go ahead...find safe ground,' I tell Jack. 'You're more heavily burdened...'

I feel the way with my feet for a few steps to the glinting water where the shape of Butters splashes and curses. My right foot sinks into soft ooze that seems to have no bottom. Pulling free, I fall onto my hands in a stand of reeds.

'Over here!' cries Butters.

'Almost there!' I right myself and find a solid tussock to set down my basket. I feel for footing, brace my feet in the reeds and reach for Butters. Our arms aren't long enough, our hands miss.

'Still sinking!' His voice holds an edge of panic. 'Don't have as far to go as the rest...'

I take off my doublet. Then I strip off my pale linen shirt.

'Can you see my shirt?' I hold it up, a headless ghost.

'I can bloody see you as well! For all the good it does me!'

'Try to grab a sleeve.' I throw the shirt, holding it by the other sleeve. But the shirt tangles and falls short.

233

I throw again.

Miss again.

I weight one cuff with a clod of mud and throw again, gently, as intent as if drawing a bow.

I hear a tiny splash. Then louder splashes.

'Got it!' shouts Butters.

I haul, hear a seam begin to tear.

Butters grunts. 'Pull...'

The mud releases him with an obscene sucking noise. He chokes and spits. His legs splash. I feel him writhing like a fish on the end of a line.

'Keep pulling. I can't swim...!'

I pull gently, the weight of Butters balanced against the tearing seam.

Butters reaches up, grabs my outstretched hand and climbs onto the suddenly-crowded hummock. In the dim light, he looks like a swamp creature made of mud.

I put on the wet shirt and doublet again. 'Forgive me.' I scoop him up under one arm. Seizing the basket, bent almost double, I bound unthinking from hummock to hummock in miraculous flight. Then I slip, curse, fight to release a foot from sucking mud, jump again. Again I travel through the air over mud and water, Butters begins to slide from my grip.

'We're over here,' calls Jack at a distance. 'Walk along the fallen tree.'

I look around in the semi-darkness. Then I see a long pale line drawn across the mud and water. With Butters clinging to me, I balance along the fallen trunk of a dead tree. The others wait anxiously on higher ground. I set Butters down.

'Well, we're even on favours now,' he says.

Though the sky has lightened, the sun still lies well below the horizon. The dogs still bark in the distance.

I climb the steep bank ahead and stumble onto a road, no more than two wheel ruts. The others scramble after me. This time, Jack turns to Olivia for directions, but she stares at the ground.

Butters gazes one way, then the other. He looks behind him at the lightening horizon then points to the right along the track. 'At least, we can see the way.'

We are in flat, wet country. Even on the track, water and mud slow us. We halt just long enough at the first ford to wash off the worst of the swamp mud. The long scabs made by the whips have been rubbed from my back. Jack smooths numbing ointment on the welts and re-dresses the now-swollen dog bite, then dresses the scratches and scrapes of the others.

We wade more shallow fords, fighting for footing among unseen stones, and cross a deeper river on a crumbling plank bridge. We slip past three homeless men stirring in their sleep under hedges.

'Are we going the right way now?' asks Jack anxiously.

Olivia marches forwards without answering. Butters shrugs. 'At least we're no closer to the dogs.'

It's now early morning. A fierce wind blows. When the wind dies, the rain begins. Soon huge puddles on the track force us to step from hummock to hummock of sedge along the verges. We are all soaked to the skin. When a finger of wind touches her, Olivia shivers in her ragged shawl and silk dress. Even the wolf trots disconsolately at my side.

I pause yet again to listen for the dogs.

'...at first light,' Jack had said. The men with dogs would be setting out, refreshed by food and sleep, unlike their prey. Unless we are very fortunate, they will soon pick up the trail we left on the track. I weigh staying on the track against striking off across the fields. But if the dogs have my scent, it makes no difference which way we go. Our only hope is speed. And luck.

The rain turns to drizzle, then stops. The sky lightens further but remains dull grey. The homeless men under the hedges must be rousing. Labourers will soon be heading for the fields. With full light, even on a grey rainy day, our group will stand out from a distance in such flat country, whether on track or field.

'Keep going on the track for speed,' Jack says, speaking my own thoughts aloud. 'But travel by day as well as by night for as long as we can.' He glances at Olivia. 'And we must change the way we look. For a start, Olivia needs a female chaperone.' He disappears behind a stone wall.

I scrub wet dock leaves on the nettle welts on my shins. The wolf lies down and begins to worry at fleas.

'Repacking my bags,' says Jacobina's voice. 'Now, if challenged, I can say I'm Olivia's companion.' She steps out from behind the wall, wearing a bodice, a skirt without petticoats, and a linen cap over her cropped blonde hair.

'I feel more like myself even if it is easier to walk in breeches.' She glances at me. 'I get to choose. One of my gifts.'

I am thinking about her words when the wolf stops and stiffens. I turn my head towards where it is looking.

The distant dogs have begun to bay after us in earnest. The doctor, the farmers or the people of Cambridge – it doesn't matter which. The day's pursuit is on.

Olivia keeps walking along the track.

Jacobina frowns. Even her calm good nature is beginning to fray.

'We're still too easily recognised,' says Butters. 'Even after Jack's transformation.' He smiles sourly. 'Mud-hopping is all very well for you with your long legs. I won't survive much more rough ground even on the edge of the track. I'm slowing you down. Leave me.'

I take off my basket pack. 'I'll carry you.'

The others tuck the contents from my basket into their packs and pockets. Butters hesitates. He mutters something inaudible.

'Be quick,' I say.

At last he climbs into my basket.

Under a grey blanket of low, water-filled clouds, we set off again. Dob walks at Olivia's side. A little behind them, Jacobina and I walk together, with Butters curled invisible in my basket. So long as Dob keeps his head down, Butters stays out of sight and no one peers too closely at Olivia's fine silk gown, we might pass as two ordinary, if dirty, couples. From time to time, I am joined by a wolf-like dog. No one shouts, 'Freaks! Traitors against nature!'

I listen to the distant dogs, imagine the men following the dogs. Their need to stop and rest. Then, up to my knees crossing a ford in a peat-coloured stream, I am hit by such hunger and weariness that the gentle current almost pushes me over.

# 16

The water gurgles past my legs. We have been walking all day, on the run from the doctor's house for most of two days and a night. This coming night will be our second one without sleep. We have rested only while the chicken cooked, it seems like a year ago but was only the night just passed. The weight of Butters pulls at my back; the basket rubs on my whip stripes.

'We must keep going as long as the dogs do.' Jacobina stands in the shallow water, skirts hoicked up, listening, too.

A bell in the far distance announces evening prayers. Unseen ducks mutter towards sleep. The dogs still bay in distant pursuit.

Jacobina and I risk catching up briefly with Olivia and Dob to confer.

'Twenty thousand, three hundred and eighty,' Olivia announces, counting steps. '…Eighty one…eighty two….' She has started to limp.

'It will be dark again before long,' says Jacobina. 'The men will surely want a dry sleep and hot food. The dogs must stop soon.'

Dogs or no dogs, Olivia and Jacobina are near the end of their strength. The ball of my left foot has blistered.

*A few more steps...and another one.*

The light fades.

Then, silence.

'Our pursuers are steaming in front of a fire, no doubt, and eating a hot meal and sleeping in dry beds,' says Butters from my basket. 'Perhaps all that water has worked in our favour as well as almost drowning us.'

'Perhaps.' I listen again.

'We can't go on without another rest.' Jacobina is white-faced with exhaustion. Dob looks determined, as if he will go on walking forever, however tired he may be.

'For a short time, while the dogs are silent...' I say.

We leave the track, united in urgency, and find cover in the scrub and trees on a low ridge of relatively dry ground. Dob and Olivia collapse side-by-side between two bushes, not quite touching, like two carved stone figures on a tomb. Jacobina shakes out her cloak. lies down and becomes a damp cloak-wrapped heap. Butters climbs awkwardly out of the basket, stretches, stamps his feet. He flattens a nest of sedge and rolls up in his cloak.

'I'll stand guard.' I'm talking to myself. The others are already asleep. I settle cross-legged with a view through the leaves to the distant road. I don't know where the wolf has gone but know he will find us wherever we are.

Nothing man-size moves on the road nor anywhere else.

I fight off sleep by listening to the frogs and owls. My ears track the tiny rustlings of night creatures in the woods around us. The rich scent of a fox approaches and veers away. My eyes cross with the effort of staring into darkness. The ghost of Kat leans against me. I turn my head to inhale the scent of her hair. The next I know, a faint light is brightening one edge of the thick mist around me. The others look as if they have not moved. Olivia snores gently. I jolt into full waking.

I squint at the rising sun. I turn my head. Listening.

A robin. A warbler. Two gulls circle overhead and give raucous cries. Otherwise, the early morning air is silent. No dogs.

Thinking hard, I wake the others.

Dob notices the silence of the dogs at once. 'They losht us in the bog.'

'Perhaps.' Jacobina is listening too. 'Or perhaps they're making a late start...or waiting for another pack to join them. Whatever the reason, we must take advantage of the delay. There's no food left, so we might as well start walking.'

Butters climbs into my basket. Still wiping sleep from our eyes, we set off with empty bellies, re-joining the two wheel tracks.  But then the marked way turns to the southwest, back towards the dogs. Olivia does not waver. She turns the other way. We hesitate then cut north-east across fields again, following her. Then our way is blocked.

Olivia seems unworried.

'What's happening now?' asks Butters's muffled voice from the basket. 'Is it safe to look?'

The channel runs fast and deep below us. It flows from our pursuers on the left towards the sea on our right. Cut into the land by man to drain away the flooding seawater, its cliff-like banks offer no gentle slopes, stepping-stones or shallow ford. Six gulls watch us balefully from the far bank.

I shift the basket with Butters on painful shoulders. 'Even the strongest swimmer would be carried away.'

'And who can swim?' demands my basket.

Below us, two ducks splash in to land and spin away on the current.

Jacobina looks down at the fast-flowing water, then towards the sea, across which I'd come from Amsterdam, to our right. 'I reckon we're nearly at the east coast. If we don't get across this channel, we either stay here or our pursuers will drive us until our backs are to the sea.'

'In other words, we're trapped,' says my basket.

I can't imagine being taken again and put back in chains.

'If Seabright Hall is across that water to the north...' Jacobina begins to draw a rough map in the earth with a stick. 'A town would have a bridge. But, if we use a bridge, we risk being seen...' Her stick hesitates. 'In any case, I don't know where the nearest town lies from here...'

Butters rests his chin on the rim of the basket. 'In other words, we're lost.'

Perhaps this is the moment. I should give myself up to save the others. I must forget that Kat assured me I am not a werewolf. I must forget what the others said when we stopped to cook the hen. I might still be guilty of killing Alice Brinkley even though every fibre of my soul resists admitting it.

My stomach rumbles from hunger at the remembered chicken. Base and noble together, I think ironically, like water and dirt trampled into mud.

Olivia snatches the stick from Jacobina's hand. She rubs out the map on the ground with her foot and re-draws the curve of the English coastline. She points east towards the coast. 'Sea'. Then she turns back  and jabs a small deep pit in the dirt. 'Cambridge.' Another pit to the right. 'Boston.' She draws a firm line, seeming unaware of our gaping mouths as she then points at the water channel. She makes five tiny, shallow holes beside it, close to the water channel with Cambridge far behind us. 'Fifty fingers. Fifty toes.'

That's us,' says Butters.

Olivia adds a sixth dot.

The wolf.

Dob points at the tiny holes in the ground just below Olivia's line for the water channel. 'We're here! She knows!'

'It's the map on the doctor's wall,' says Jacobina in awe.

Seeming not to hear, Olivia sketches a light broken line from our group of tiny dots, away from the sea. She points at a small muddy path leading to our left, back towards the dogs. We risk starting them off again.

'We should follow that path? Turn away from the coast?' I ask. 'But that's the wrong direction.'

She looks at me silently.

'Is there a bridge?'

Without hesitation, she draws a long straight line on the far side of the channel. The she draws a matching line on our side.

'That must be an old Roman road,' says Jacobina. 'It must cross the channel.'

Olivia's stick touches the light broken line just before the water channel, near the Roman road. Our path. She draws a faint line across the channel.

My soul jubilantly says that there's perhaps no need to give up yet!

'Are you certain there's a bridge?' Butters asks.

Impatiently, ignoring his question, Olivia draws the channel widening towards the sea. She prods more deep pits of villages into the earth-map. She draws a web of roads and tracks. It is a careless demonstration of her skill. I can do so much more than the ridiculously little that you need of me, say her actions.

She points again at the narrow muddy track shown by her broken line. Then to her faint line across the channel near the Roman Road. 'Bridge,' she says firmly.

'She could not have seen that map more than once,' says Jacobina. 'It's one of her gifts!'

This time, Jacobina and Dobb follow her without question.

I hold back, still puzzling at what is eluding me. I look at the wolf for help, but it is absorbed in killing a flea with its teeth.

Olivia, Jacobina and Dobb keep walking away along the narrow muddy track.

'Well?' Butters rests his chin on the rim of the basket and raises his brows.

'The morning's well-advanced and the dogs are still not barking.'

'We lost them in the swamp, as I said. Hurrah!'

'Perhaps.' The silence worries me even more than the sound of dogs, though I can't think why. Pursuit, I understand. Sudden silence, I do not. After a moment, I swing the basket with Butters up onto my shoulders and follow the others. The wolf licks its jaw with a long black tongue and trots at my hip.

A lock gate stands open in the channel. Beside it, a fragile bridge hangs suspended from pilings driven into the banks. One at a time, carefully, we cross. I cut the ropes suspending it. It crashes and clatters against the far bank. The fast-flowing current now lies between us and our pursuers. They can rebuild the bridge or try to move the open lock gates, or try to go around the channel, but they will need time that we can use.

Once across the channel, we turn east again, towards the sea and Amsterdam. Behind us the channel flows into the Wash, whose waters grow broader as it opens into the sea that I remember crossing on my way to England. At each branching of ways, we follow Olivia. The wolf appears and disappears but always finds us again.

The grey blanket of the sky lifts. Patches of blue peek between white pillow clouds with sagging purple bellies. The land grows even flatter. Sometimes, it seems to be as much water as earth.

We reach the coast near sunset on our third day on the run, when the sun is burning a low orange slash through the clouds in the western sky. The open silver water of the Wash now lies far behind us, cutting inland back towards where we crossed the channel. We turn north along a long, flat beach, half brown mud, half-sand. The occasional wet stone gleams like polished steel in the failing light.

Our footprints overlay the delicately etched tracks of wading birds with both short and long curved beaks. Jacobina leaves male-sized prints. No dog would make paw marks as huge as the wolf's. We are leaving a clear trail. Clear enough for Kat to follow if she gets that far.

Then I see that the tide inches upward. In two more hours, it will erase all footprints. And their smell. Dogs will not be able to follow us either.

Then I realise what has been bothering me all day about the silent dogs.

I still have not decided what to tell the others when we climb a high, grass-covered earth bank at the far end of the beach. Seen from the top in the growing dusk, the bank stretches ahead of us along the coast like the back of a giant green snake. To our right lies the bumpy brown mud and twining channels of salt marshes and skeins of grey-black sea. To our left, the glint of water-filled drainage ditches stitch together the land.

Excitement mixes with terror. We must be standing on the sea wall that my grandmother described, built to hold back the hungry sea from the low flat fields of the estate. It is just as she said. All we need to do now is follow the sea wall until it leads us to Seabright Hall. If I can recognise it.

But before we arrive, I must warn the others.

'Is that it?' Butters points through the dusk to a tiny light far to the west.

'Too far inland. "The sea wants to swallow up its fields," my grandmother said...' I must tell them why I am dawdling.

Dob clambers down the left side of sea wall and starts collecting reeds. The rest of us watch him curiously and sink down into the darkening grass. Dob climbs up again and shows us how to gnaw the pith of the reeds.

I must tell them. There's no hurry.

Sleep ambushes me.

When I wake in the clear, early dawn, the infant day feels fresh and new, like the first morning of the beginning of the world. Dew sparkles like sequins on the edges of the reeds below me. Water shimmers on both sides of the sea wall. My wet clothes have dried. The wolf is stretching its forelegs, hindquarters in the air. I forget for a moment that I am a freak of nature wanted for murder.

Sitting in the grass, I feel my eyes reach out to touch the horizon across this great, flat sea of the earth under an immense bowl of sky. The fresh tang of salt marsh tickles the back of my throat. I sniff the dense aromas of rotting seaweed and dead fish on my right and the sweet heavy cloud of may blossom that rolls over us from the land to my left. The rich scents make me feel drunk. The 'gift' of my new powers of smell and hearing – Jacobina's words begin to make sense.

If I could only always just travel like this, I think. Kat at my side. Never arriving.

The wolf sits down in front of me and looks into my eyes. I lay my hand on its head. 'Give me courage,' I beg.

The others begin to stir. The moment can't be put off any longer.

'Wake up!' I say roughly. I am not good at giving bad news. I squat down and draw a deep breath. 'I need you all to listen to me.'

'What's wrong?' Jacobina is instantly alert.

'I must go on alone.'

Butters lets his large head drop heavily back onto his arms. 'I knew you'd change your mind about us.'

'I understand the silence of the dogs. I may be leading you into a trap, must have blabbed to someone. They don't need the dogs any longer.'

'Are you asking me to give up the chance of a real bed?' demands Butters.

'It's me they want, not you! You're on the run from a madman who wanted to kill you. But being with me will convict you too.'

'...And I'll be happier when we all stink less of dirt, smoke and sweat,' Butters adds. He glances at Jacobina and Dob.

'The men in the posse chasing us may go straight to Seabright Hall, wait for me there,' I insist. 'Not because they lost our scent in the swamp. By now, they will have learned the name of the estate. They tracked me just long enough to know where I must be going. You all risked your skins once to rescue me. I won't let you to do it again.'

'Let me choose for myself,' says Jacobina. 'I'm coming with you,'

Dob nods silent agreement.

'Are you withdrawing your earlier invitation?' asks Butters.

'No, but...'

'Then I'm coming with you, too. But I hope you don't mean to carry me again. I'm not too old to walk.'

One more thing bothers me, though I do not tell them: I told Kat about Seabright Hall. She might have been the one who blabbed.


I don't need the peals of church bells that ring from the circle of steeples. I know the place, just as you instantly recognise someone you have not seen for a long time. I point at a geometry of distant walls that rises from the flatness. 'Seabright Hall.' I am certain.

I study the sea wall, the fields, the pattern of water-filled dykes (not sea-walls against water as in the Netherlands but channels for water), the distant brick walls. I study them again. No tents are visible anywhere in the distance, no fires, no movement of any kind.

I listen to the encircling ring of bells. Pride swells unexpectedly in my chest. My past – my true self – was not, after all, an old woman's wishful maundering.

Dob points out the distant house to a sleepy Olivia. 'We're going to live there!'

We watch from hiding in the long grass as the sun climbs. The posse that pursues me is very patient, or else not there at all.

We continue to watch, unmoving in the grass while the sun passes its midday peak and begins to slide into afternoon. Still nothing moves below us. Butters scowls at the low clouds on the horizon. 'More rain before night. At least we might have a roof over our heads!'

'Perhaps,' I mutter. I stroke the wolf which has trotted back from a private exploration to be certain that I'm still following, however slowly. I look into its eyes for guidance. I wish I could send it out as a spy. It lies down but remains with its head lifted, turned to the estate. After a long look at it, I decide to watch a little longer.

We gnaw more reeds. I daydream about food. The wolf sets its rusty muzzle on its paws.

'There!' I murmur to Jacobina. A flicker of movement among the distant walls.

We watch intently for a long time. It is not repeated. The wolf sleeps.

A bird or animal, I decide.

As the sun continues to drop, we risk moving closer. The wolf rouses, trots with us and lies down in the new spot. We sink into the grass and watch again.

Still no signs of life. No fires. No men-at-arms.

Suddenly, I can't contain myself. I begin to run with the half-empty basket jouncing on its straps. The wolf lopes at my side. Headed for my rightful place on earth, where I belong. The others scramble down the grassy ridge of the sea wall after me.

After crossing two fields, I skid to a stop. The wolf looks up at me in question. The others catch up. They gaze silently across the thistles and mud.

I had let myself be fooled by distance. 'At least we won't have to fight any residents.' Perhaps the posse pursuing me had already heard and dismissed it as the place I might be heading.

What had looked from the top of the sea wall like open gates in the estate walls are gaping, ragged holes.

From here, I can see how heaps of brick rubble replace sections of the outer wall that once enclosed the big house, outbuildings, and orchard. Inside this outer wall, more broken walls outline the house itself. Tilting hammocks of collapsed roof hold pools of rainwater. Dark, empty eye-sockets stare back at us in place of glass windows. Lumpy, over-grown, green-black yew trees sprawl among the nettles and dock in the former gardens to the left of the house.

'No feather bed for me tonight,' says Butters sourly. 'Your estate's a sodding ruin.'

My face burns with shame. I had let myself imagine Seabright Hall just as my grandmother remembered it, with her painted ceiling still in place, as if fifty years and King Henry's armies had never been. It is now clear that, once wrecked by the king's men, Seabright Hall, the home of traitors, had been left to rot. Only two seagulls squabbling on a sloping roof ridge disturb the desolation.

Jacobina drops her heavy case and stretches her back.

A flock of birds rises from the field in front of us like leaves blown up by a gust of wind, then settles again a little farther away. Olivia counts the birds, not interested in

either ruined house or our sudden change of humour.
'One hundred and seventy-two,' she announces.

My shame ebbs. I straighten my shoulders and sniff
the wind that carries salt from the marshes. I smell the
heavy, creamy sweetness of May bloom and the sharp
lemony scent of the grass crushed beneath our feet. Ruin
or not, this place is mine. My rightful place on earth.

'Our good fortune! Where better could we escape
attention?' says Jacobina.

Its desolation soothes me. The flat, flat land – my
land – under the huge, arching sky has a bleak beauty. In
that vast space, my problems shrink to insignificance.
Their hush suggested that the others feel the same.

The eerie whistle of wings throbs in the air. We lift our
heads as a flight of swans passes overhead toward the
salt marshes and the sea beyond.

'A good sign,' says Dob. He watches Olivia's face and
her interested, searching eyes. 'A good place. I can
help...' His hands draw an imaginary wall rising in the air.

'Nine.' Olivia watches the swans fly into the distance.
'I like this place,' she says to no one in particular.

Desolation. Beauty. Grandeur. Privacy.

And it belongs to me. I will not have to prove that the place is rightfully mine, because no one cares to dispute it.

I reach down and lay my hand on the scruff of the wolf, which stands at my side, muzzle raised, testing the air. 'Delicious new smells, eh?' I point at a small brick outbuilding. 'That one still has its roof. We'll sleep there tonight under cover for a change. Tomorrow, when not so weary, we can decide what to do next.' I already know that I want to stay here at any cost.

We pass through a gap in the outer wall, headed for the ruined house along a narrow track between ancient, gnarled apple trees shaggy with grey-green lichen, just coming into bud.

A growl rumbles in the wolf's throat. I smell a man's rage behind me. The wolf's warning saves my life. As I begin to turn, the blow glances off the top of my skull rather than smashing it. Face first, I hit the ground.

# 17

I shake away jagged lines of colour blurring my sight, hear a groan. Dob lies flattened beside me. I sense movement and roll to my left. The earth shakes with a thud where my head has just been. Olivia screams, '*No, no!*'

A giant looms over me, a length of heavy timber raised to strike again. I lurch to my feet, half-running, half-falling, knowing that the next blow will break my back. I will be helpless. Death will find me just when I have found my place on earth.

The giant bellows.

My feet catch up with the rest of me. I spin around.

The giant has dropped the timber. He claws at Butters, whose legs are wrapped in a choking grip around the tree-trunk neck. Butters throws one arm across the man's eyes, blinding him. Then he hooks two fingers of his other hand into the man's large nostrils and yanks upwards as if trying to pull off his nose.

The giant begins to punch blindly at the air. I hear two blows smack on flesh. Olivia still screams, crouched against an apple tree, hands over her ears. Jacobina struggles to hold the snarling wolf by the fur of its neck.

I look for other attackers. Hear another smack of fist on flesh and see Butters flailing through the air.

Then the wolf breaks free from Jacobina and leaps at our attacker's throat.

'No!' I shout. I fling myself at the wolf. The wolf's teeth close on the back of the giant's brown leather jacket. Its claws scrabble for purchase on the man's huge legs.

I grab one massive arm and cling on. Dob catches hold of the man's other arm and is swung off his feet. The giant tries to shake us off, twisting and bucking violently as if we are hounds that have closed their jaws on a bear.

I feel the wolf slam against me. Then I am flung the other way against the wolf. Ground and sky whirl around me. I am being shaken by the mastiff. My spine will snap. The wolf will close it jaws in a new grip and tear out the man's throat. Death will flood the ground.

'Stop!' I try to shout, but the air is jolted out of me. I cling on, unable to breathe. There is no end to blood and death. Every growl and heave further destroy our possible safety at Seabright Hall.

'Hold him steady!' yells Jacobina. With loud grunts, Dob and I dig our heels into the ground. Jacobina lifts her skirts and knees the man in the balls.

Shouting in agony, he takes me, Dob and wolf to the ground with him in a flurry of fur and flesh. I kick, feel my foot connect and roll onto my feet. I grab the wolf by its bristling neck and pull it away. 'Leave him!' The wolf strains forward, russet muzzle snarling, yellow incisors bared like curved knives.

The giant groans then pushes himself up onto his knees. He eyes the wolf, still rigid, teeth bared, in my tight embrace. Then his eyes slide to the piece of timber nearby on the ground.

'Leave it!' Jacobina points the pistol at his head.

I look around. He seems to be alone. No posse. I suck at the air, boiling with anger. "Why did you attack us? Who the devil are you?'

Butters joins us, brushing mud from his clothes. He glares at the man he has attacked. 'Never again! That was absolutely the last time!'

'Speak! Or I'll set the wolf on you,' I say.

'No one comes here…unless they mean mischief.' The giant pants for breath. He plants one foot in front of him, watching both wolf and gun. Slowly, he heaves himself up to his full height, enormous in the slanting rays of the setting sun. 'There's nothing here for you.'

He is about eight feet tall with broad shoulders that could pull a plough without horses or an ox, and a wild grey beard and wilder hair. Two streams of blood run from his nose to his upper lip and drip from his chin.

'Nothing here left to steal,' he says. 'What the king left, thieves and nature finished off! So shog off all of you...Mistress Pistol and all your friends. And you...' He looks at me. '...take your vicious beast with you.' Though big, he sounds human enough.

I keep one restraining hand on the wolf's nape. As tall as I am, I look up into the man's face. 'This is my house. The estate belongs to my family, the Seabrights. And I asked who you are.'

The fight has cracked open the healing whip stripes on my back and the wound on my head. The pain feeds my anger.

The giant wipes his bloody nose on his sleeve. 'Your house, my arse! Any beggar brat could make that claim. D'you think I'm newly hatched? '

The wolf strains forward under my hand, vibrating with a low growl. I clench my other fist. 'I'll ask just once more: who are you?'

'Live here, don't I?' The giant waves a ham-like hand. 'Have done for fifteen years. Found the place abandoned. Nobody cared a tuppence for it. Repaired things, didn't I? Earned the right to live here! You see that outbuilding over there?'

He points at the roofed brick shed where we intended to sleep. 'That's my forge – where I make an honest living as smith for neighbouring farms and estates. I sleep there, too, and don't care to share my bed with a bunch of rag-tags escaped from a travelling menagerie.'

Without warning, he charges at Jacobina and wrenches the pistol from her hand. He points it at the sky, pulls the trigger and then looks closely at the powder hole. 'Didn't think it was loaded. A rum bunch you are! Don't try to cozen me, my friends, because I mean to stay here!' He hefts the pistol by the barrel like a club, ready to break a skull.

'This is my house and my estate,' I repeat fiercely. 'My family have owned the land for seven generations. I'm

Rafe William Seabright, the only survivor in my family and rightful heir to Seabright Hall.'

Cold eyes rake me up and down. 'Prove it!'

# 18

'Stay in front of me where I can see you, all of you.' The smith shoulders two spades and his length of timber like guns, the empty pistol now in his belt.

I lead off through dock and thistles across a field beyond the lichen-covered orchard, steering for the two remaining walls of a man-made structure in the far corner of the field.

The smith swivels his eyes at Dob, Butters, and Olivia, then back to me and the wolf trotting at my side. I watch his eyes rest a little longer but no less thoughtfully on Jacobina's long stride.

Silently, I repeat my grandmother's instructions. Let me remember them accurately… Let them be right! What if my demon soul-wolf will not let me touch a holy object? If I cannot prove my ownership, what then? The giant smith will fight for possession of the estate. With his size and strength, he might well win, even against us all.

And if we win?

We can't kill him. I want to clear myself of murder, not commit it.

We reach the two crumbling walls. The remains of a large sheep shelter lies half-hidden by grass and weeds. The once-thatched roof has fallen in. Collapsed beams crumble like peat. I let out a breath of relief. 'We dig here.'

I hear the smith throw down the two spades. Jacobina gives a grunt and then a wheeze. When I turn, I see that the smith holds her pinned in front of him in the embrace of his massive arms like a chained bear about to crush a dog, the length of timber clutched in one fist. 'Anything I don't like and I will break her ribs till they stick out of her back!' The smith squeezes harder. 'Don't make me hurt her.'

I clear the quarter of the floor least littered by fallen beams and begin to dig with one spade. Dob takes the other. Butters piles our clods outside the collapsed shed.

'Digging for treasure?' asks the smith with a sneer, over Jacobina's head.

'Yes,' I say shortly. I stop to pull my shirt away from my back, which had begun to seep. My palms are already blistering. Jacobina stands quietly in his crushing grip, snatching at the air in short gasps with the top of her chest, eyes willing me on. I give her what I hope is a reassuring look.

The smith turns his head to spit into the grass. 'I've heard of your sort. Scavengers...vultures. Makes a change from robbing graves, I suppose.'

Olivia now sits a short way off, seeming to ignore us, watching two crested grebes ducking in an out of the reeds at the edge of a water-filled ditch. The wolf has vanished on explorations of its own. More than ever just now, I need its physical presence to anchor me.

When the hole grows to three feet deep and four feet wide, I stop with one foot on the spade. I never asked my grandmother how deep to dig. What if I give up a finger's width too soon? All our futures depend on finding what I am looking for.

I dig again.

Water begins to seep into the hole from the surrounding soil.

'Nothing will be buried deeper,' I mutter to Dob. He nods his agreement.

Feeling the weight of all their eyes, I clear and begin to dig up another quarter of the floor.

'How long will this proof of yours take? I want my supper.' The smith wipes his bloody nose and beard on his shoulder without loosening his grip on Jacobina.

My spade hits something hard. I fall to my knees and dig with my hands like a dog. My fingers meet a hard corner.

Carefully, with my hands, I dig out a long shape wrapped in damp, rotten linen. Under the linen is a layer of oiled cloth. I unwrap the cloth to reveal a heavy fluted column mounted on three curved legs. A silver candlestick, now blue-black as if charred in a fire. Not what I am looking for but getting close.

'What does that prove?' asks the smith over Jacobina's head.

I scarcely hear. A thought has just hit me.

My father may have held this candlestick.

The boy who became my father had almost certainly helped to dig this hiding place... had helped to carry the family treasures from the house to be buried here. My grandmother had shovelled in the dirt that I've just scraped away with my hands. I close my fist on a clod of earth.

I'm back.

It is a strange thought. Makes no sense at all, but it feels right.

I see the smith looking at me curiously.

Dob now digs with renewed excitement. Rotten cloth wrappings fall apart in our hands as we find tarnished silver spoons, more candlesticks, pewter tankards, blackened silver plates, knife blades whose wooden handles crumble away in our hands. But not yet what I seek.

'Forty-eight spoons,' Olivia announces. She is watching us, after all.

Butters jumps into the hole. He disappears. Then he pops up, shaking the dirt out of a brass bed-warmer turned blue-green with *verdigris*. 'This will warm my sheets on an icy winter night.'

'People who flee are bound to bury the things they can't carry,' scoffs the smith. 'Proves nothing.'

Butters sets the warming pan in the grass and disappears into the hole again.

'Haven't found my proof yet.' I keep digging with my hands.

The wolf returns and lies down beside the hole, ears pricked forward with interest. It watches me intently.

Butters pops up again. 'Here's real treasure – flint fire starters!' He glances at the wolf and ducks out of sight.

Carefully, I scrape away the earth from a bundle of rotting linen the size and shape of a swaddled new-born babe.

I prod it fearfully.

No demon soul-wolf recoils in horror. I lay my hand on it. 'I think this is my proof.'

The smith cocks a disbelieving brow.

I set the bundle in the meadow grass so all can see clearly. 'Are you content that I have not dug in this place before? And could not have seen what is in this?'

The smith sets his jaw. 'Not to my knowing.'

'Yet I shall now describe this object to you. My grandmother's most prized possession.' I swallow an unexpected lump in my throat. 'Though she grieved to leave it, it was too heavy to carry, and she could have been killed merely for having it.'

I close my eyes, holding tightly to her description lest it slip away as my name had once done. 'Inside this rotting cloth is a crucifix. With the Four Apostles on the base, all made of gold. Golden vines twine around the stem of a golden cross, as if a living tree were holding up the Son of God. The cross itself stands on the blue dome of the Heavens.'

The others listen with wide eyes as my words decide their future.

I begin to unwrap the rotten linen.

Inside the linen is oiled cloth. Inside the oiled cloth is silk as fragile as a breath, which falls apart under my fingers. Then more oiled linen, and more silk. I unwrap a last strip of oiled linen. And there it is.

My proof. Unseen by me till now. The Seabright Crucifix. The four golden saints, unspoiled by time: Saint Luke, Saint Mark with his lion, Saint Matthew and Saint John, each in a garden of gold. The enamelled blue dome of the heavens that arches above their golden heads has also defied time. It is the half shell of a magic bird, bluer than the sky, blue like a magic jewel. Every detail is just as grandmother described. I take the crucifix in both hands.

Time shimmers. For a moment, I am eight years old again, running along the edge of a sea far away on the other side of the grey water. I listen to my grandmother tell of an unknown, mysterious England that waits to welcome me.

'This once stood on the private family altar here at Seabright Hall. I promised my grandmother that I would set it in its rightful place once again.'

I have found it. We are safe.

Then I hear Jacobina gasp. Sweat beads the smith's broad forehead. His grip has tightened. His eyes are filled with desperate indecision.

I am not thinking clearly. We are not safe at all. To the smith, who lives here alone, I and the others have just become a worse threat. I have just proved myself the rightful owner of the estate. The smith will have to surrender control. At best, these odd-looking strangers will invade the smith's quiet, solitary life. We would give orders. Or else we might drive him away. At worst, these strangers, whom he has just attacked, might kill him.

I watch the man think it through.

If the smith manages to kill us all, he could lose our bodies in the marshes. No one would ever know we had been here.

'The estate needs a good blacksmith if we are to put the place to rights.' I glance at Dob who nods in swift agreement. 'Nails. Knife blades and hammer heads...'

'Horse shoes,' says Dob.

'Bridle bits.'

'Weights for scales.' Jacobina adds breathlessly.

The smith glances around our group. Warring thoughts chase themselves through his eyes. Kill them... don't kill them.

His arms tighten; Jacobina gives me an urgent look.

I grab at words. 'You were right to defend the place against a rag-tag bunch like us...grateful that you did, in spite of the lump on my head.'

The smith closes his eyes in an agony of indecision.

I force a smile. 'I bear you no ill will and hope you bear me none.'

Jacobina snatches a breath. 'You make things...make...not a destroyer.'

The smith looks down at her, startled.

She takes another tiny gasp of air. 'I'm certain...you are gentler than...you would have us think.'

The smith breathes in and out in a great gust.

He must have loosened his arms a little. Jacobina speaks almost full voice, though her agitation shows when she slides into the naturally deep tones of Jack. 'Don't alter your true nature from...misplaced...fear of us.'

Slowly, she pulls the massive forearms looser but makes no move to escape. 'We are gentle, too, once you grow to know us. We can all live here in peace.' She heaves a deep grateful sigh and turns in the slackened grip. 'That's better.' She looks up at the smith's face. 'We must find some clean cobwebs to staunch your bloody nose.'

'You a physician?'

'Of sorts.' Jacobina smiles up into his eyes. 'And grow herbs for your cooking pot.'

'And who knows what else, eh?' The smith looks past her at me. 'Is this a trick? I won't be driven off!'

'You have my word,' I say. 'We need your forge. Please stay to help us.'

The smith glares at me for a long moment. Then down at Jacobina in his arms.

We stand unmoving. No one speaks. I hear my pulse beating in my ears.

The smith lets his arms drop. Jacobina takes several deep breaths but backs only two feet away, still within his grasp if he wishes.

He crosses his arms over his broad chest. 'Now that I take a good squinny, you've the dark-haired look of your family.' He holds up a broad hand in warning. 'Before you ask, I've seen a portrait that survives in someone else's parlour...just don't expect me to call you "young master" and whip off my cap to you.' He sniffs through his large nose and wipes it on his sleeve. 'And don't hold your breath waiting for me to say "welcome".'

Jacobina and I exchange glances. This is not the moment to tell the smith that the new master of Seabright Hall is accused of being a werewolf and murderer and might be arrested at any time.

If only matters were different! I could grow like that golden vine. Reach full manhood, marry Kat, father her children...

I set off back to the ruined house with the crucifix cradled in my arms, pockets filled with spoons and firelighters. The others carry as much as they can. Even Olivia has been given a bundle of cutlery by Dob. The rest will wait for us to come back with bags.

The smith collects the spades and follows us. The earth trembles with each step he takes. 'Well, Master Seabright, I hope you're not too much of a gentleman to labour in the fields. You'll have to, if you hope to make anything of the place.'

If I am given the time.

'In spite of the new Scottish king's reputed tolerance,' I ask to cover a storm of emotions, 'isn't it dangerous to thrust rich, probably Papist things like this under other people's noses?' I gesture towards the crucifix with my chin.

The smith shrugs.

Butters snorts as he walks. 'How is it any different from thrusting us under people's noses?'

The smith gives the little man a thoughtful look then gazes around the group again. 'There's sweet water on the estate as well as brackish. I cleaned the well.' He pauses, swallows. He reads enough kinship in us to offer at least temporary hospitality. 'I've fresh-caught fish. Preserved goose and barley porridge. Goat's milk cheese. You can sup tonight anyway.'

'Have you room for us all to sleep in the forge?' I ask.

The request seems to strain the hermit smith's newly born, if reluctant, good will. We take several more paces before he replies. 'I repaired the roof in a room of the big house. You'll all fit there.'

I nod agreeably. It is a handsome offer for a man who has lived alone for so long.

'You might manage to find a small space in the forge just for me, by your fire,' persists Butters. 'My old joints need warmth.'

The smith looks down in sour amusement at the little man who trots at his side. 'If you trust me not to smash your ugly head in.'

'I'll risk anything for a good night's sleep.'

# 19

The smith builds a peat cooking fire in an old iron cauldron outside the forge. He guts several of the fish he keeps alive in a barrel. I place the Seabright Crucifix on top of a broken wall. As I watch the first flames leap up into the sky, the world spins around me. The invading demon soul-wolf suddenly crouches a few feet away.

Please, not now!

Dizziness and confusion take me over. The fist rises up in my gullet.

I turn blindly to the shadows, my back to the fire. The fist of terror sinks back into my belly. My soul-wolf retreats. The real wolf lifts its head from its paws and looks at me in question. I put my hand on its nape and close my eyes. After a moment, my calm returns.

I force myself to look at the flames again, jumping against the sky. The ball of terror starts to rise again in my gullet. Sounds become sharp-edged and clamorous. My demon soul-wolf comes closer, jumps onto my shoulder. I feel the odd shift of skin and muscle begin.

Quickly I turn back to the shadows and close my eyes again. No, I say silently, no!

After an unknown time, my soul-wolf retreats again.

I remember the juddering torches of the farmers and my confusion...the back-lit priest. Even thinking about them invites the soul-wolf to come nearer. The juddering torches...forcing myself to look at...The realisation remains solid.

I suddenly see: the 'demon' wolf comes in leaping flames. Shadows and darkness are safe places: comfortable, peaceful shadows and darkness. I do not seek darkness because I am a devil fleeing the light. I need dark because it is quiet, and its quietness subdues my internal wolf.

I test this version of the truth by looking quickly at the flames and turning to face the shadows with renewed relief. I sit breathing quietly, face turned to the dark. I need time to let it sink in.

Stillness and darkness heal me.

I haven't rid myself of my soul-wolf, but now I may have some idea how to tame it.

But if I am not a werewolf, don't transform, don't threaten, what happened to Brinkley's daughter Alice?

I stand up restlessly and wander into the darkness of the ruined house. Men still pursue me for her murder. Seen over my shoulder, the group around the smith's cooking fire eagerly watch the flames die down for cooking. For my part, I have lost all appetite.

I want to talk to Kat about my discovery about my soul-wolf, want to discuss Alice. I want to talk to Kat here at Seabright Hall among my new friends and allies. I want her to see me in my rightful place, no matter how much work it needs nor how briefly I am here. I ache to let her know that I was not trying to impress her with empty boasts. I long to tell her that she had been right all along. 'I will never harm you!' I would say.

I rub a clenched fist against my forehead. Where is she now? In prison? My mind stumbles at the image of her being recaptured and beaten by Grillet. She should not have stayed on Grillet's estate to help me...should not have fled with me...the dogs have her scent as well as mine.

I rub my forehead again. I had abandoned her, let the doctor push me down into hiding under the blanket and left her behind in Cambridge. How can I imagine that she would want to be with me?

The wolf stands and growls; its muzzle points into the falling darkness. I hear what it hears. I raise a hand to quiet the group around the smith's fire.

'Someone's coming!' A boat. Water drips from muffled oars.

My other hand feels for the hidden dagger strapped in my boot. A boat thumps against a wooden pier hidden by trees.

The smith reaches for his club. 'I'll deal with them! The rest of you take cover.' He steps to the centre of the space in front of the fire. Dob and Butters come to stand at his side.

I push Dob and Butters back. 'Let me give myself up.'

'You, too!' says the smith. 'I've dealt with outsiders before.' He lifts his club over his head. In the firelight, he is terrifying.

'Rafe!' a voice calls. 'If you're there, hide! They followed me.' A burdened figure climbs up from the water-filled dyke, breathing hard.

She wears breeches and a wide-brimmed hat.

'What's going on?' the smith demands.

I leave the dagger and step past him.

She spies me. 'You're here after all! I've been trying to find you ever since you left Cambridge. Had the devil of a time finding Seabright Hall. Your directions were terrible. Kept heading for the edge of the world. Thought I once I was about to fall over it.'

Kat. In men's clothes, blonde hair stuffed under a hat.

'You found me.' Even in male clothes, even with that haircut that looks like a badly mown hayfield, which I can see now that she snatches off her disguising hat, she takes my breath away.

'Clearly, I found you! Or else I wouldn't be here, would I? And just as well. I keep saving your life, don't I? The posse is coming after you, following me... hasn't heard...'

The wolf growls again more loudly. I hear movement from the direction of the sea wall behind us. Then more boats bump against the wooden pier through the trees in front of us. I smell the reek of men's fear.

"They're already here!' she whispers.

'It's a madhouse!' says the smith.

Men close in from all sides. They approach from the sea wall and from the direction of the water. The firelight glints from drawn swords.

A large, thin man with lank hair steps from behind a pile of bricks. He points a pistol at the smith's head. 'Drop that club.' His voice trembles with hope that he will be given the excuse to shoot.

'No peace!' cries Olivia's voice. 'No peace.'

The smith's fist tightens.

'Don't be a fool.' I say. 'The estate needs you alive.' Quickly, I raise my hands and step into a clear space by the fire. 'I think you seek me.'

'No peace!' Olivia repeats.

'The one who *calls* himself Rafe Seabright?' sneers the man with the gun. 'I arrest you for murdering and eating a child.'

'Alice Brinkley has been found alive.' Kat says.

'A-live.' I stammer. 'But...'

'Just said as much, didn't I? That's the latest news to reach Cambridge.'

The militia volunteers who surround us clearly have not heard that Alice is alive and are frightened by arresting a youth accused of being a werewolf.

'You heard her!' I say.

'Take him!' the militia leader orders. 'You can count on villains protesting their innocence!' He is rewarded by grim smiles from some of his men.

'Alice Brinkley has turned up uneaten and in one piece!' Kat insists.

The man is not listening. He has locked eyes with the smith. His finger trembles on the trigger.

The wolf growls. Dob moves towards me.

I jerk my head back toward the shadows. 'A noble gesture on my behalf won't help Olivia!'

I think Dob understands my risks as well as I do, but he is still poised to fight.

'Go on! Bind him!' orders the man with the gun.

'He wouldn't have done what you say!' The smith ignores the pistol, which points from him, to me, and back again. 'Master Seabright there is a gentleman! A landowner returned after years of travel to reclaim this estate by right of birth. What kind of homecoming welcome is this?' His words take wing. 'From old local family! Owns the very earth you're standing on. Will become our Member of Parliament, *Sir* Rafe Seabright.'

Butters is climbing a pile of bricks.

'Well, I was told that the child is dead! Go on! Bind the child-killer! As for you, you overgrown freak of nature, shut your mouth or we'll take you too.'

The smith shifts his grip on his club.

'No!' I warn.

Butters stands on a broken wall, poised to jump, eyes fixed on the leader.

"Don't!' I hold up my hands desperately to stop him.

'BIND HIM!' the leader shouts.

I step forward. 'Don't do anything to help me!' Dob, Butters, the smith and the wolf must not join in. 'It will become a fight, one of them may be injured and then we will all be lost.'

Dob, Butters and the smith hesitate.

Four men approach me warily. Two are roughly my size and weight. One of the others, is smaller but wiry. One outweighs me, most of it muscle, a square bulk reminding me of the mastiff. A fifth man stands ready with a rope. Not good odds.

'Save the worry of guarding him!' the leader shouts. 'Hang him now. Find a good strong branch...'

'Will it be safe?' asks one of his men.

'You are quite safe to arrest me, if you insist.' I shake my head desperately at my little would-be army. 'I haven't killed anyone!' I hold out my hands as if to be tied before they can search me. I am lying down and exposing my belly to a larger dog, but my behaviour lies.

If they look for a hanging tree...orchard most likely...I will pretend to stumble, seize the hidden dagger from my boot and kill as many of them as I can before they hang me. If they take me to a boat, I will fling myself overboard when far enough away from the others to risk the inevitable shooting. Dead is dead. It doesn't matter. Shot or drowned. I will not be chained in darkness again. Nor can I let the others, including Kat, risk their lives for me again.

'I'm trying to tell you she's alive!' Kat shouts to the leader of the posse. 'With all her limbs still attached in all the right places. He's a hero, not a murderer!'

'Are you the one we followed for the last two miles? The leader stares at her. 'Is that creature a man or a woman?'

'You left Cambridge too soon,' she says. 'You've been charging bravely after him all for the sake of a dead hen. Should hear the ballad they're singing about you now! *"Here come the mighty wolf hunters with their prey in chains..."'*

'Take her, too,' orders the leader. 'And the big one. Take the split muzzle animal too, while you're at it, and the imp!'

'No peace!' screams Olivia.

The smith swings his club in a circle around him.

*'"...wasted all their pains..."'* sings Kat defiantly. A militia man seizes her by the arm. She claws at him with the little curved knife hidden in her hand.

Dob launches himself at two of the militia men. Butters jumps from his pile of bricks onto the neck of a third.

Olivia begins to scream without drawing breath.

'I'll soon tell you what she is!' shouts one man. Two militia men wrestle Kat to the ground. One pins her hands while the other one begins to undo her belt.

'Rafe!' she screams.

Rage boils up in my belly. Men grab at me. I shake them off, past thinking. Lips drawn back in a snarl, I yank a man off Kat and fling him sprawling. I hit a second man, the large one, behind the ear with both hands, fumble for my hidden dagger.

Brick chips explode from a wall. The acrid smell of black powder fills the air.

'Dangerous men!' screams Olivia. 'Dangerous men!'

The man sees my face, tries to crawl away. I catch him and take a fistful of his hair to pull back his head. Dimly, I hear hoof beats. I smell the horse before I see it. I freeze with my fist clenched in the man's hair.

'Stop!" a man yells.

# 20

His horse skids to a halt between two piles of rubble.
'Jack! Sam! Stop!' the rider shouts.

I unclench my fist.

Olivia still screams. The enraged wolf drags Jacobina
along the ground towards me as she clings to its neck
with both arms. She digs in her heels and manages to
stop it in its charge, its incisors still bared. The horse shies
away from it.

I lower my dagger. I almost killed a man. Came close
to murder for real. No going back from there. My legs
begin to shake. 'Steady, boy,' I say to myself as much as
to the wolf. The militia men hover.

The rider keeps his seat but takes a moment to
steady his horse. 'Which of you is George Foxton?' His
horse sidesteps farther away from the wolf.

The posse leader raises his free hand; the pistol still
smokes in the other. 'We've caught the creature that
murdered and ate Alice Brinkley. And arrested his
accomplices. Not that it's any business of yours.'

'I have here an arrest on this posse, by names, to cease on pain of confiscation! Naming you George Foxton as leader. Alice Brinkley has been found alive. Hiding, frightened of her father, I'm told.' The horseman unbuckles the pouch strapped at his waist and produces a folded document with dangling red official seals.

'I told you!' Kat stands up and glares at her attackers. She re-buckles her belt.

Olivia stops screaming.

'We'll see who's official and what's what when we get back to Cambridge. Bind the child-killer as I ordered!'

'I warn you,' says the man on horseback.

'Let me see that arrest! Have I seen you before?'

'Very likely. I'm Will Triplow, one of the night watch of Cambridge – and official courier.' The rider leans and hands the arrest to the posse leader. 'Is that official enough for you? I'm sure you'll recognise Magistrate Wardlaw's signature and seals.'

'Have care, Foxton,' warns one of the men. 'Wardlaw had my cousin's ears cropped last month.'

Foxton studies the seals and signature closely by firelight. 'I suppose we must believe this,' he says at last.

'I would advise it,' says Triplow grimly. 'And, Foxton, I have a special message for you. Your dame says to come home at once – none of your usual excuses – to finish the shearing, or you know what will happen.'

Foxton's men suppress smiles.

'How did you know where to find us?'

'Easy enough. You left a string of happy, gossiping innkeepers behind you.' His horse side-steps a little farther from the wolf. 'Then you took to boats and headed straight for Seabright Hall...the young man's name, after all.' He turns to me. 'Thank the Lord, I met a farmer who had heard of the ruddy place! Took his advice and followed the top of the sea wall...I should let him go, if I were you.'

The members of the posse regard their leader in consternation. The dangerous adventure has turned to an embarrassing mistake that could cost them dear.

'Leave him,' mutters Foxton.

'I told you to think twice!' booms the smith. 'Master Seabright may bring a case against you for wrongful arrest. *I* might!'

I hold out my hand. Foxton passes the arrest to me.

'That farmer Grillet looks a fool for calling out the dogs for what turns out to be a mere hen.' Triplow seems to be enjoying himself. He gazes around the militia men. 'When it comes down to it, you're a Cambridgeshire posse out of your home county here in Lincolnshire.'

I press my fingertips against the red seals, the signature, the names of the posse. I let out a long breath. I turn to Kat. 'Are you all right?'

She nods.

'You came to find me!'

'To give you the good news that reached Cambridge at last. Alice Brinkley has been found alive, hiding from her father, just as I said! Didn't want a beating. And he jumped to conclusions, like those farmers!'

We both stand a little dazed, as if rocked by a physical blow. I gape at her, mouth working like a hooked fish.

'Alice is alive,' I repeat. It is still sinking in. Jacobina was right not to think I transformed. Dob and Butters were right. Kat had been right all that time ago. I had been right in my deepest feelings.

'I didn't kill her? I don't transform?'

Kat shakes her head.

My soul-wolf invades me, beyond doubt, but I have some idea what brings it. I am not a monster werewolf who kills and eats children. I am dangerous only to myself. And to the ignorant and superstitious. I am in danger from their ignorance and superstition.

'Who knows the true story?' I ask.

'Everyone. Who matters, at least.' She picks up the bulky object with which she was burdened. 'And since I took the trouble to bring you this, I might as well deliver it.' It is a lute case.

'No one thought to tell me...' the smith begins.

'Alice Brinkley is alive? The search for me has really been called off?'

'They've taken down your placards in Cambridge. And the ballad seller's had to change his song. Didn't you hear me? Go on! Take it!'

The smith looks from me to her and back again.

Beyond words, I take the lute case. I feel the brush of her hand. She snatches her hand away and hides both hands behind her back. I want to grab them.

Instead, I open the lute case. I lift out a bent-necked lute. I exhale in awe and delight. I turn it in the firelight. Ebony and ash wood, striped cream and black like the finest lady's gown. I touch the delicate lace of the carved wooden rose set into the flat top under the strings. 'Where did you get it?'

'Never you mind!' She wraps her arms around herself. 'Now that I've delivered it and the good news, I should move on...'

I pluck a stream of notes like water drops falling in the sun, the round curve of the lute's belly settled against my body. She must surely hear my joy even if I cannot speak it.

'Lute!' says Olivia.

Kat turns her head to the girl's voice and nods as if confirming something to herself. 'I should be on my way,' she says again, more firmly. But she stays where she is, not moving, looking at me.

My fingers go still on the strings. In the silence, I hear the snap of the glowing coals. A distant sheep bleats.

'Don't go.' I bend my head closer to the lute, hiding my face.

'Do you want me to stay?' She nods towards Olivia.

'I may not have killed Alice. This posse...' I lift my head and look around at them. '... is dissolved. But there is still danger to all of us here – you'll soon see – from people who are afraid of us.'

Two militia men look away, unable to meet my eye.

'You would ask me to stay?' she repeats. 'If there were no danger to me?'

It is just turning real. I am no longer pursued for murdering a child. I have begun to tame my soul-wolf though I do not understand it. Kat has come looking for me. I raise my eyes to hers. Our shared intensity will drown me. 'I need someone to keep saving my life.' I lay the lute carefully to one side and grab her hands at last, but then don't know what to do with them. 'I'm free! It's finished!' A whoop of joy forms in my chest.

'Didn't I just say as much?'

The smith clears his throat like a millwheel beginning to grind. 'I feel there's something you've not yet told me.'

'I have a…' How best explain what I do not understand myself? 'I am sometimes not my ordinary… I've been falsely accused of doing vile deeds while…' Falsely! I want to howl and sing. To turn somersaults but that would mean releasing Kat's hands.

'Do you mean you're mad? You become a risk to be around?' The smith begins to look dangerous.

'Neither,' Jacobina interrupts briskly. She still holds the growling wolf by its nape. 'Master Seabright's trouble is more like a passing megrim, needs only a brief rest in the dark. No worse than having too much drink. No worse than most of us.' She measures the smith from head to toe. 'Less evident to the eye than some.'

'It always passes without ill effects,' adds Kat.

'Lucky man, to have such fair and eager advocates.' The smith eyes me for a long moment. 'Is there any other circumstantial lie, or lie direct, that you want to confess while you're at it? Before I make a fool of myself by introducing you to the world as the new master of Seabright Hall?'

'No more lies of any sort,' I say.

I become aware of the discomfited posse. Giddy with love and relief, I play the country gentleman to the hilt. 'Gentlemen, if you're no longer going to arrest me, my hospitality is yours. Such as it is.' I glance at the smith.

'Must get back,' one man mutters. '...this time of year...'

'At least dry yourselves at the fire. Have something to eat before you go.'

Triplow dismounts. 'I'll stay till I'm sure these men are setting you free.'

Foxton leaves at once, silent and head down, taking with him the five men in his boat. I watch them disappear into the shadows towards the boats. He will be an enemy from now on.

The six who came in a second boat bring their heads together in a cluster of hats. They confer: they would indeed like to dry out before going back. And, perhaps, a little food would also be acceptable. I see the gleam of their curious looks under their hat brims at the smith, Dob, Butters, Jacobina, Kat, Olivia, the wolf and me, undecided about our unusual group. But they also accept the official word, whatever it may be at this time. And they are hungry.

'Then I'll build up the fire and get on with gutting more fish for our guests.' The smith thuds away. 'Any more of you out there lurking for free food?' he bellows to the night.

Once Foxton has gone, Triplow goes too, with apologies for not staying for supper.

Kat brushes dirt and leaves from her breeches. She keeps brushing.

I watch her study our group beneath lowered eyelids: the giant smith; Butters the child-sized man with greying hair, who has elbowed his way to the fire between two of the militia men; Jacobina with hair cropped like a boy, strong hands and deep voice. Dob with his split muzzle like a goat. The wolf. All of them prepared to fight for me.

Her eyes rest a long time on Olivia, sitting apart from us all ignoring us again, face buried in her arms while Dob makes soothing sounds and strokes her back.

Kat catches me looking at her. 'Sorry. Didn't mean to call you for help...'

I want to say, I'm glad that you did. But the words don't seem quite right.

She covers her discomfort by eyeing the wolf which approaches us, now free of Jacobina's embrace. 'Last I knew, you wanted to tear all traces of a supposed wolf from your being. Now you keep company with a real one?'

'I've accepted some things.' The wolf brushes against my thigh while I give it a reassuring scratch. Then it moves behind her and breathes hotly through her stockings as it sniffs her legs.

'I assume we're safe with it.' She stands very still.

'It's deciding whether or not to bite.' I'm only half in jest.

We hang in time while the wolf sniffs her legs. I feel as if I'm waiting for the rest of life to fall into my hands or be snatched away.

The wolf bumps the back of her legs in a friendly way, looks at me and lies down by the fire again.

'You've passed its inspection.' I try to smile. 'Have we passed yours?'

'Are you asking the spawn of the devil to presume to judge?' she asks lightly.

'Life here with me...with all of us...will have its risks. This evening won't be the last of it, I'm certain. Someone else will hear about the "freaks of nature" at Seabright Hall.'

'Are you asking me to live here with...all of you?'

'None of us bites,' Jacobina says. 'We're people in spite of appearances.'

'Let the young woman eat before you insist on answers,' says Butters. 'Or at least, let me eat! The matter is too weighty for an empty stomach.'

Prompted by Butters, the smith begins to serve aromatic grilled fish on thick trenchers of bread to everyone including the militia men. They look curiously from me to Kat while they pretend to be absorbed by eating. Except for Olivia, who ignores us all.

'There's a lot to be done here at Seabright Hall,' Kat observes.

I watch her mouth as she swallows a piece of fish.

'We don' mind hard work.' Dob returns to chewing on a comb-like fish spine.

Kat assesses the shadowy ruins. 'Rebuilding must start at once if we're to be ready for winter.'

I think she has just agreed to stay.

But on what terms?

The smith speaks into the sudden silence that follows her words. 'Finding enough food...don't know... Fish, of course. Plenty of those. And eggs from the chickens I recaptured from the wild – survivors of the original flock, I imagine. And the orchard still bears fruit in spite of its age...' He stops, embarrassed by his rush of words.

I take her wrist and lick the fish juices from her fingers. Then I bite gently on the side of her palm. She holds my eyes as my mouth and tongue taste her skin. Her sweet sweaty scent again fills my nose. I want to bite down but resist.

I open my jaws. 'I'll never bite you harder.' I can say it now. I know that it's true. Whatever I am, I'm not a werewolf. I did not kill Alice Brinkley. I'm no longer pursued for that crime.

She looks back at me levelly. 'I'll take my chances.'

I bury my face in her palm for a moment. We sigh in unwitting unison, hear ourselves and laugh with shared delight.

Butters begins to clap sardonically. 'A happy ending at last. Must say, you two took long enough!' After a pause, he is joined by three of the militia men. The other three become even more interested in their fish.

'I've never learned how to behave as part of an "us",' Kat warns. 'You must give me time to grow used to it. It feels strange but good, like beautiful new shoes that have not yet eased to fit your feet.'

The fire has burnt down to non-threatening coals. I can look at all my new friends around and across the smouldering embers. I pick up the lute. After a moment of feeling the strings respond to my fingers again, I play four bars and raise my brows at my companions – I feel at home with them. Not alone. There is power in our union – are we not here, alive, filled with shared intent?

301

Olivia watches me.

'*Under the greenwood tree...*And a one, two, three...' My voice is clear and true.

'*...who loves to lie with me?*' Jacobina is the first to join, in a deep alto voice, singing 'la, la,' where she can't remember the words.

The smith begins to rumble like summer thunder.

Butters says, 'I can't sing!' but then makes musical sounds that encounter the melody from time to time. Dob hums under his breath until he has found the melody then improvises around it like a bird. The militia men chew their fish bones. Then one begins to tap his foot in time to the music. Another listens for a few bars and begins to sing in a deep baritone.

Olivia turns her head from one to another.

'*Here shall they see no enemy but winter and rough weather,*' we sing. True for the moment, at least.

Kat joins us in a high, true soprano.

The wolf's throat trembles with the beginnings of a howl. A suppressed sound emerges like the faint murmur of an underground stream.

Olivia begins to rock in time to the music. 'Sad sounds, frightened sounds, dancing sounds, happy sounds.'

I think about the night to come.

Kat's voice twines around mine, vibrating with it like a single string. Suddenly, she presses both hands to her mouth as if to hold in tears or a shout of joy.

The wolf raises its head, opens its throat, and joins the song.

I don't need to understand more. For the moment, all is well.

PLEASE READ CHRISTIE'S MESSAGE BEFORE
YOU CLOSE THE BOOK:

# From the Author

This is the most important book I've written. These characters are real and living today. I know because I am one of them. I am a non-supernatural 'werewolf'. We just call them by a different name.

I began to wonder how many other people besides me experience life in ways that are classed as fantasy, imagination or neurosis by people (including doctors) who have never had that experience. Then I began to wonder about historical 'fantasy'. Was it so fantastical? It became necessary to write a 'real' version.

In *Fur Beneath the Skin,* which is an historical novel, I call people by the old historical labels like 'changeling', 'imp', 'devil', 'giant', 'wizard', 'hermaphrodite' and 'werewolf' as used in the period when the book is set - the early 17th century (the Jacobean period which followed the Tudor Elizabethan). But I had my characters think and act truthfully, to the best of my ability, just as their modern equivalents might have done. This freed my imagination in a new way that I have never seen before.

The current general treatment of werewolves, vampires and other fantasy creatures is to deal with them as separate issues. They are mixed together in this book. I have chosen to do so because it is faithful to the period when *Fur Beneath the Skin* is set. Then, unlike now, issues of diversity were lumped together in a moral and religious bundle. In the early 17th century, medicine and science, including alchemy, were just beginning to catch up with modern thinking.

I started writing with Rafe the werewolf and my own experience, but I go on to show how diversity embraces all differences of all kinds. Diversity goes beyond race and religion to include differently-abled and gender assignment. It does not change the human being inside. It does not change with centuries, whatever you call it.

Possible modern, 'medical' labels:

**Rafe. A 'Werewolf'** has focal epilepsy, a form of epilepsy that does not cause total loss of consciousness, or 'falling' as in 'falling sickness', but does cause memory loss of the near past, along with 'hallucinations' of smell, or pain. First defined only in the 20th century as part of a range that includes epilepsy and migraine, its symptoms can often be misdiagnosed.

I have focal epilepsy resulting, as his does, from a head injury. Rafe's experience of transformation, of 'wolfishness' is mine, although it is just one of many possible manifestations of focal epilepsy.

Like Rafe, I have groped for memories. Like Rafe, I have heightened senses which persist beyond seizures. Like him, I've sniffed with delight. I'm lucky to have been let off relatively lightly. I've never had my purse and clothes stolen, for example; I've had to imagine those from other people's experience. I've learned to live with the fear and ignorance of others and to accept the gifts – the heightened senses - of my condition as well as the downside.

In a footnote in his book of essays *The Man Who Mistook His Wife for a Hat (1985)*, the neurologist Oliver Sacks first confirmed for me a possible tie between focal epilepsy and historical werewolves. Though writing about a boy who thought he was a dog, not a wolf, he says, '...it was the exaltation of smell that really transformed his world.'

My epilepsy first started when I was thirty-two. From the very beginning, I was confused by conflicting advice (and still am). I began to write my way out of this confusion at 3:00 am in the emergency ward in hospital. I thought about the names throughout history for the fearful, fantastic or assumed-to-be mythological – and decided that they weren't so mythological after all. Then, released from hospital, I researched. I learned that between 1 and 10 of us out of a hundred fall somewhere on the migraine-epileptic spectrum with accompanying altered sensations – one to ten per cent of us. The total number of young people affected is astronomical, whose experiences differ from what is generally defined as 'normal' by psychologists and doctors. They have had their physical and emotional experiences dismissed as imagination, delusion, hallucinations or neurosis.

As well as Rafe, the werewolf, *Fur Beneath the* Skin also sheds modern light on the following:

**Olivia**. **The 'changeling'**. Likely to have been high-performing autistic. The age for diagnosing autism is roughly the same as it was for changelings - around two years old – and the symptoms can be similar, like not speaking, or speaking your mind without a filter, or total recall of certain things. She might now be luckier in her parents and diagnosed as a high-performing autistic and be encouraged to develop her strengths. In *Fur Beneath the Skin,* total recall is the one singled out though others are implied.

**Dob**. **The 'devil's child', with a split muzzle like a goat**. He would now be diagnosed with an oro-facial cleft, or cleft palate. In *Fur Beneath the Skin*, in the 17thc, he was banished to sleep in a barn where he learned the language of animals. If born today in a well-off society, Dob would almost certainly by adolescence have had restorative surgery and be barely noticeable.

**Jack/Jacobina. The 'hermaphrodite'** would now be called 'gender-ambiguous' or 'gender-fluid'. An openly discussed (but not until the late 20th c) but still hotly debated percentage of us lies somewhere between the definitions of clear-cut male and clear-cut female. Hers is only one of the many ways this ambiguity can exist. Her preference for living as a woman is shared by two of the writer's gender-ambiguous friends. Another trans-gender friend has chosen to transition both chemically and surgically and embrace his male soul and body even though her body was defined at birth as female.

The word 'homosexual' was first defined in the 19th century, long after the time of this book. Same-sex love and practices did exist in the 17th century (as they did before and after), but they were thought to be purely moral issues. They did not define identity as they more often did in the 19th, 20th centuries and do in the twenty-first.

**Butters, the 'Imp', or 'dwarf'** and **Smith, the 'giant'**. Equality laws now bolster their on-going fight against size-based prejudice. A very few of them might even become leading actors in popular television series and films. Acceptable vocabulary changes.

**Kat**. '**The spawn of the devil**'. A bastard. No longer necessarily a shameful thing to be. Not being able to read didn't mark her out in the 17th century when many people could not read. 'Dyslexia' had not yet been heard of and was not mentioned until the 20<sup>th</sup> century.

In the past, people feared what they did not understand. What they feared, they tried to destroy. Today, we destroy and do damage in our own way. Even if we don't like to admit it, we often secretly fear those who are different. We don't burn them at the stake, but we distance them. We pass well-meant laws 'to protect them' that draw attention to difference. We call in doctors, police or social services. We often give differences medical-sounding names, with negative-sounding 'dys-' or 'mal-' or 'psycho-' stuck on. We prescribe therapy or drugs or surgery or send 'sufferers' to special institutions. We write articles about them. We tie ourselves in knots trying to use language that won't offend while accurately describing reality.

Whatever these differences are now called (and I stand by my modern re-classification), they add up to a lot of teasing and bullying including trolls on the Internet - to a lot of secret fear. I am not talking about extreme cases, where parents and other carers are called on to be heroic beyond belief. I am talking about the thousands of cases of children who are excluded from school, the young people who know they are different, silently feel shame and have no one to talk to.

Like Rafe, Jacobina, Dob, Butters and Olivia, I am one of many outsiders but not supernatural. Though we, the different, still fight for a place in the world, communities of acceptance are growing. It doesn't take magic to explain us.

You may have a friend like one of them. Could it be you?

See difference, not defect.

See and respect another person.

You can make a difference.

***– Christie, a friendly werewolf***

THAT REALLY IS THE END

Rafe & The wolf

Rafe meets Kat          3·10

Threatened with Exorcism.  3·02

Rafe and The wolf    16

Exorcism.
end of my bit over to Christie.

werewolves.
            heightned Senses.

Rafe Kat

Rafe & The wolf

Christie.

Lightning Source UK Ltd.
Milton Keynes UK
UKHW021840311020
372564UK00012B/75